"The ... together, Carla,"

Kyle told her. "I don't know what He has planned for the two of us, but that's where faith and trust come in, you know."

"If only I could be as sure as you are, if only I could feel as though—"

"It's forgiven," he interrupted her. "It's forgotten. That's the answer. Take ahold of it, hold it tight to you. Our faith stands or falls on forgiveness bestowed upon us by a holy God."

"But you have no idea, Kyle, of my past...all that I've done," she whispered.

"Quiet, Carla," he soothed her softly. "As far as I'm concerned, it didn't."

"But it's true. You can't pretend—"

"It's not pretense at all," he told her, showing as much patience as he could muster. "When God forgives our sin, He isn't pretending. As far as He is concerned, none of it exists. It's been washed away."

ROGER ELWOOD

is a bestselling author in the Christian book market with over twenty titles to his credit. He has won twelve awards for Best Book of the Year from the Excellence in Media Association. Roger has also been named as a finalist for the ECPA Golden Medallion Award. The trade editions of his bestselling Angelwalk series have sold nearly a half million copies to date, and each of the four titles has appeared in top positions on the CBA bestseller lists.

Formerly a resident of the East Coast, Roger now lives in Agoura Hills, California.

Promises
Roger Elwood

Published by Steeple Hill Books™

STEEPLE HILL BOOKS

Steeple
Hill™

ISBN 0-373-87008-6

PROMISES

Printed in U.S.A.

"...weeping may endure for a night, but joy *cometh* in the morning."

—*Psalms* 30:5

The supreme happiness of life is the conviction that we are loved.

Victor Hugo

Prologue

 ❧

With some nervousness, Carla Gearhart glanced at herself in the makeup mirror which was ringed its entire circumference by soft-ray bulbs that provided light but little glare, and illuminated every part of her face. A long time had passed since she dared to examine her reflection in this manner, afraid that she would look so weary, so prematurely aged that no amount of makeup would compensate. Yet she realized that, somehow, she actually seemed younger than she had just two years before.

That fact was why she continued to stare at the image as it really was and yet questioned whether she was simply deceiving herself, precisely what she might have done at another time, another place.

Lord, surely this is not real, what I am seeing. Surely I've got to be fantasizing, she thought. *After all that has happened, all that pain, those long hours of doing nothing but worry and cry, how in the world could I look this good?*

But the mirror was not deceiving her, nor was she deceiving herself.

Her flame red hair was healthier looking, and a bit longer

than before, flowing like a river of molten fire that bordered on iridescence—the once deep-set circles under her eyes, evidence of a life lived recklessly had vanished. Her skin glowed, her complexion having lost a certain paleness, and she could also actually count *less* wrinkles, crow's-feet and the like, not more, a self-analysis that surprised Carla with its results.

Lord, I have been to hell and back! she exclaimed, *and yet the years seem to have fallen away from my face. I looked older than this the morning after I won my Oscar for Best Actress of the Year.*

One hand happened to be resting on a relatively new red leather-bound Bible, the other on a gold-framed color photograph of a young man in his late twenties, square-jawed, with a slight scar slicing through his left eyebrow.

Older....

He looked older, over thirty in fact; his shirt off, showing a chest that was muscular but not grotesque, more like that of a champion surfer than a body builder.

I suspect that that was the problem, she told herself. *If you had appeared as young as you truly were, I doubt that I would ever have—*

Carla stopped that thought, suspecting all too well that there was no way she could have predicted anything about their relationship because, after all, he would have been the same person he was regardless of his age, and nothing about her would have changed except perhaps her expectations.

How she did love this man! How wise he seemed!

Though only half a dozen years older by the calendar, Carla Gearhart was much more than that in terms of her experience in a life that had had more peaks and valleys, it could be said, than much of Switzerland itself.

"By contrast, you seemed to have lived like a monk in some monastery," she said out loud. "And that innocent, modest manner of yours. You were so different from any-one I'd ever known."

Kissing...

A flashing memory of his lips touching her own took her back to the first time they had held one another.

We were standing on the deck of a riverboat that was cruising down the Mississippi toward New Orleans, Carla remembered. *I told you I felt nervous about the performance I was scheduled to give there and I told you I had prayed about it. And you stood back, and looked at me as though you were seeing me for the first time, then you leaned over and kissed me, and we stayed like that for what seemed like the rest of that little journey but which probably was only a few minutes, lost to everything and everyone around us.*

She brought her fingers to her lips.

I had not been kissed like that since high school, she told herself, *with such tenderness and even a little uncertainty.*

Carla sighed as her finger moved up to her lower eyelids and wiped away a tear that had formed.

You seemed so strong, she recalled, *but nothing like any of the other men I had known—*

Carla cut herself off, tears starting to pour in earnest down her cheeks, causing her makeup to streak.

What a mess, she told herself as she looked again at the mirror, and the sad reflection that it now gave back to her. *The makeup girl will—*

The door!

Lost in her thoughts, preferring the company of even bittersweet memories to the harsher present reality, Carla was startled when someone began knocking on the door to her star's dressing room.

"Are you okay, Carla?" the stage manager asked apprehensively. Despite himself, he had developed some affection in recent months for a woman whom he once had found quite intolerable but who now was very different, changed so drastically that some idle, jesting-type scuttlebutt was actually suggesting that she might be an identical twin who had taken on the task of impersonating the real Carla Gearhart.

At first she could not answer, hoping that he would come back later, that for the present she could be left alone.

"Are you—?" the voice started to repeat with a bit more urgency.

"I will be, Albert," she interrupted, "God knows I *have* to be."

"That He does, Carla. Bless you."

A second of silence, then: "Five minutes and you're on."

Five minutes!

Under ordinary circumstances, getting her makeup back on would take at least half an hour. How could she possibly reconstruct it in a fraction of that time, especially since her makeup girl was nowhere around.

"Are you still there, Albert?" she asked quickly, hoping to catch him before he was involved in some other task.

"Yes, Carla, I am."

"I wanted to say something else."

"Go ahead, Carla."

She could think of few times in her adult life when she was tongue-tied but this was surely one of them.

"Thank you for being a friend, thank you for your concern, though I wonder if I deserve it," she said without telling him what was going on inside her head, but meaning the word *friend* more than she had ever thought possible, since she once had been prone toward treating stagehands and assistant directors and others of their ilk as servants who had to do her bidding or she would make matters totally miserable for them.

"You never called me that before," he acknowledged.

"But I do now, Albert, and it comes from my heart, dear man."

"I'll be back in four minutes."

"I know I can count on that."

Carla glanced at that photo on the makeup table, knowing how great a part Kyle had played in her transformation from show business *haridelle* to what she had become, and speculating where she would be without him in her life.

Kyle, she thought, *my love, my impossible love.*

Carla reached out and brushed the year-old photo with her fingers, pretending that, by doing so, she could somehow touch Kyle himself, that the glossy paper it was printed on was a kind of portal, and he could be found on the other side, and all she had to do was reach through, and he would be there waiting to hold her again.

If only you were here tonight, she told herself, *if only you were in the audience and I could sing my heart out to you in front of everyone, and tell you before tens of thousands of witnesses what it means to me that I have been able to love you.*

How she hated those two words.

...if only.

It might be that they were the cruelest in the English language, forcing her mind and emotions back over territory that it might have been better *not* to revisit.

...if only.

That second time, the tears came in a flood that could have proven unstoppable but she was still a woman of exceptional will, a will that used to be so dominant that it sought to control others but which now focussed only on herself, and how badly she had treated people before Kyle and she had met. And Carla knew that she could never let sorrow and despair get the best of her, could never let visions of the past few months squander her present, for that would not have pleased Kyle, that would have upset and alarmed him terribly and brought him hurrying to her side as he begged her, "You must stop this, you must not destroy yourself. I am not worth it, my dearest Carla."

Despite her melancholy, she chuckled at that.

I am not worth it, my dearest Carla.

As she put her hand back on the Bible, enjoying the texture of its leather binding, she said out loud, "Not worth it, Kyle? God brought you into my life. If for no other reason, that makes you more precious than you could ever realize."

She picked up the Bible slowly and leafed through it, then stopped as she came to Romans, and then on to 8:28: "All things work together for good to those who know and love the Lord."

Written by Paul the apostle at a point in his life when death seemed close, a death implicit with ridicule in front of a bloodthirsty crowd of people excited by the sight of someone dying, his sentence given at the maniacal command of a gloating emperor who had sought that moment for a long time, it seemed almost incomprehensibly joyful, a grand delusion under the circumstances, and yet she was drawn to a second verse much like the first, Philippians 4:11: "I have learned, in whatsoever state I am, therewith to be content."

Another knock.

"One minute, Carla," Albert called in to her.

Her hands were trembling. In a flash she had lost her courage, and would now have to give in to her pain.

"No, I can't," she replied sadly. "I can't do this. It is too soon after all. Tell them I am not ready. You must do that for me."

Silence, for only a few seconds, but it seemed longer.

Albert asked, "May I come in, Carla?"

"Yes…"

She was not keen on spending any time with him at that

moment because she could easily guess what he would say, knew what he would try to accomplish, knew that she did not want to hear any of it. And since she was the star, she could order him or anyone else to respect her every wish—at least the old Carla Gearhart would have done that.

Albert was young and rather good-looking but Carla knew that he had survived some hard times—survived only by finding his faith.

Albert saw that her hand was on the Bible.

"Still wondering?" he asked since he knew the details of what had happened, and could understand her feelings. "Still searching?"

"Wondering? Searching?" Carla repeated. "Yes, I am, Albert. I begin to wonder if I will ever *stop* wondering."

She stared at him with a look that was akin to desperation.

"What has happened is still new, fresh," Albert added. "If you cut your arm, it won't heal in a day or even a week perhaps. Depending upon how deep the cut is, that healing might take the better part of a month. And, remember, Carla, that is a simple cut. Your pain is much more severe because the wound itself is."

"I am afraid it will never *stop* hurting," she said, her voice quavering. "How could I endure that? How could I *ever* endure that? Getting up each morning only to face—"

Carla stopped, embarrassed.

"I see you now, the way you are, as part of the good that came out of knowing Kyle. The two of you might not have met otherwise."

"That's true, Carla," Albert acknowledged. "I might have been headed straight for an eternity in hell."

"I don't know about that."

She was still uncomfortable with discussion along those lines, though the idea of hell had seemed a natural part of Kyle's faith.

"Oh, I would have," Albert reiterated. "My life was all wrong. I felt so weary more often than I could count. The drugs aged me a lot, you know. And they messed up my mind. I was dangerously close to cursing God. I know what *that* would have done to my spiritual destiny."

"We are not so different," she told Albert. "We lived, we sinned and we had to have ourselves cleansed."

"There's no past tense involved," he reminded her. "It will be a constant battle that goes on until the day we die."

Carla nodded, hating the truth as he presented it but knowing that truth for what it was, an unassailable series of facts from moment to moment.

"Will you get ready now?" Albert asked. "You've got more than fifty thousand people waiting for you out there."

Carla had been slumping slightly in her chair but that brought her up straight.

"*What?*" she blurted out. "That's capacity, isn't it?"

"And then some, Carla. Extra seats had to be brought in. If the fire department doesn't find out, it'll be a miracle."

"My biggest live audience..." she muttered.

"A record. Nobody's got that kind of draw, and you've got to be aware of that. Remember, too, that there are no supporting acts, which is unusual in itself. You're the whole show."

"Half of me feels dead right now, and yet I'm the whole show," she said with some irony.

"Now wait a minute!" he exclaimed sternly as he pointed toward the mirror. "Don't you see how you look?"

"Younger..."

"That's right, Carla. Knowing Kyle has done that to you."

Yet she scoffed at her appearance.

"I *feel* ancient."

"With that kind of attitude, you could start your slide

all over again, Carla, and find yourself in a place that's emptier and even more hopeless than you ever did before.''

His words struck a nerve and she remembered the old days, sliding from the giddy ones after the Oscar ceremony to where she could not get out of bed without drugs, nor go to sleep at night without downing a quantity of pills that could only be called dangerous.

"Kyle saw you, and look at what happened!" Albert exclaimed. "Was all that he did for nothing?"

Carla waved one hand impatiently through the air.

"All right, all right," she replied. "Give me a few minutes."

He smiled slightly.

"What do I tell them, Carla?" he asked. "What am I asking fifty thousand human beings to believe?"

"That this is my first gig since…since—"

She was starting to choke up, and Albert interrupted before she put more stress on herself.

"I'll think of something," Albert said as he stood. "Maybe I could do some kind of comedy act."

He kissed her on the forehead.

"Pray for strength," he whispered with some warmth. "The Lord will give it to you, Carla."

Then he closed the dressing room quietly, leaving her alone again.

Carla's hands were trembling as she wiped the streaked makeup off her face, and started to apply as little as possible to replace it, just enough to give her lips some color under the glaring spotlights and soften the puffiness tears had caused around her eyes.

After she was finished, she got to her feet and turned toward the door. Then she stopped as she told herself that Albert was only one of many who were expecting too much of her. Her audiences always made such heavy demands that she was bound to crack sooner or later as she tried so hard to please every man, woman and child who paid for the privilege of watching her perform.

"Forgive me, Kyle, for I just don't have your strength, I'm afraid," she said out loud as she opened the door and turned toward the exit, not the auditorium.

Empty.

That was odd. It was usually *too* busy, with people forever bumping into one another, especially as showtime approached.

No sounds, nothing except—

She stopped abruptly, listening.

A voice.

A voice that sounded distant and she had to strain her ears to hear it, a voice that was speaking her name.

Carla!

That was what the voice said, and so distinctly that she spun around to see who had come up behind her.

No one.

Shrugging, chalking it up to her nerves, she continued toward the exit a few feet ahead of her.

Carla!

There it was again.

She had heard it that second time or thought she did but still could not tell the direction from which it was coming.

"Who are you?" she asked. "Why are you doing this? Leave me alone."

Carla reached the exit door.

Don't leave, please.

"Stop it!" she screamed. "I can't go out in front of those people and pretend that I feel like *entertaining* them!"

Yet pretense had been a part of her life since the beginning of her career.

As an actress, she always pretended to be someone else when she played a role in a movie. As a singer, she was role-playing, too, someone happy and bursting with energy, someone an audience would pay to see so that they could have a couple of hours of escape from their own problems.

"I'd only garble the lyrics, get the rhythms all wrong, miss the cues, make a fool of myself," she said. "Tens of thousands of people would leave and talk, how, yes, yes, how they would talk, about me washed up, that I should have retired years before, and not tricked them into paying hundreds of thousands of dollars to sit and watch a broad like me pretend that I had no crosses to bear."

Carla hesitated, half expecting the voice to say something else immediately.

She was wrong.

Only sounds from the auditorium behind her could be heard as Albert told the awaiting thousands something that the speaker system magnified a little too loudly so that the volume had to be turned down.

"Carla Gearhart will be with you soon," he said.

Feet began to stamp in impatience and protest.

"Now I want to tell you why there is a delay," Albert continued, pausing for effect, then continuing.

She held her breath.

Albert is pretty smooth, she acknowledged. *He should be able to keep them from walking out for a little while, anyway.*

Her insides were trembling.

What about later? she worried. *What if they leave the auditorium and start spreading the word about me? What will happen to my career then?*

She was instantly ashamed of that egocentric thought, and pushed the exit door open, a winter chill hitting her cheeks full blast, feeling like a hand slapping her across the face.

An alley.

She gasped as she saw it.

An alley, a dismal, dirty alley, beset with odors that seemed more like those in a filthy rest room...

Inside the theater building were once-adoring thousands of clerks, accountants, teachers, computer salesmen, housewives, many others, along with the requisite bright lights, glitter at every turn, however fake it might have been, as well as all the other aspects of a million dollar engagement.

Yet outside—

None of this was unusual except on Broadway perhaps, and even in that fabled district of Manhattan, derelicts managed to hide briefly behind trash Dumpsters or use sections of each alley as not-so-private outdoor rest rooms.

Oh, God, Carla thought prayerfully. *This is where I'm headed if I don't stop myself tonight. Oh, God, I need Your help! I can't end up this way, my guts eaten up by drugs or maybe in a cheap motel, dying after taking a hundred sleeping pills.*

A filthy back alley seemed a metaphor for what her life would have been like without Kyle Rivers—dark and filled with all manner of trash and with no real hope that any of this would ever change.

Go back inside....

That voice!

She pressed her palms against her ears but it would not stop since she now realized that it seemed to be coming from *within* her.

Kyle loves you, Carla. Whatever happens, remember that. And don't give up. That's what the enemy of your soul wants.

She answered instinctively, pointing out the sheer ugliness of that alley, and its putrid odors.

"Yes, I *know* that he loves me," she spoke. "And I love him enough to know that without him in my life, what do I have left? This is where I could be someday, eating scraps that others have thrown away."

God is with you.

"Sounds like an old story, often repeated," Carla retorted sarcastically. "Isn't there anything new to say?"

She clenched both hands into fists.

"Why give me hope, and then snatch it right from my grasp?" she begged. "Why show me my true love and—?"

Never mind any of that, Carla. You must go back inside and trust God. Without trust, your faith is a charade.

But still she resisted though less certainly, taking one step, then another away from the stage door and down the alley toward the street beyond it.

Suddenly she saw movement.

A middle-aged derelict had pushed aside a pile of cardboard boxes under which he had been sleeping. In his hand was an old rusty trumpet.

Carla walked faster, a bit afraid because she was well dressed, obviously "from money" and he was a typical panhandler. Normally these people, she had heard, were not violent but then desperation was a wild card in anybody's life.

She was almost at the end of the alley, just a few feet from the street outside.

"You can just walk 'way and leave everythin' and everyone behind you," the derelict spoke. "I can't. I's stuck where I am, can't do nothing about it."

...you can just walk 'way and leave everythin' and everyone behind you.

Carla stood still. Suddenly she could not move.

Her band.

She was leaving every member of it behind her, betraying them along with fifty thousand customers, part of that great mass of people who had made her the success she was.

How can I do this, Lord? she prayed. *How can I stab them in the back like that?*

She took one more step toward the street.

The derelict let out a cry of despair that hit her like a very large block of ice, chilling, it seemed, every nerve in her body.

Slowly Carla turned, and saw him standing in the middle of that alley, and seeming very much a part of it, as dirty, as smelly, as filled with debris but his trash was different, for apart from his wretched clothes, it was inside him, the refuse of a life that apparently had been inexorable in driving him to that alley that night. She walked back into the alley, and approached him, standing there, wanting to say something but not yet quite sure what the words should be.

"Hey, lady, what are you starin' at?" he snarled defiantly, having learned the bad habit of being offensive to everyone.

"You," she told him honestly.

"What about me? You ain't seen no bums before?"

"None with a trumpet in one hand."

He looked at it, and chuckled as he said, "You got that right, lady. I'm one of a kind I am."

"Why are you carrying it like that?" she asked.

"Only thing I got left from the old days. I never let go of it. I'll be buried with it, yes, ma'am, I surely will."

"You have played the trumpet professionally?"

"Shoot, lady! I was tops years ago. Lookin' at me now, you's probably thinkin' I'm dreamin' or somethin'. But I ain't. Gene Krupa, those other guys, they were no better than me, no, ma'am, they sure enough weren't."

"Do you have any family left?" Carla asked, aware that scaring him by talking about his eternal destiny would only have made him shut her out.

"Not any more. All dead, or so disgusted with me that they might as well be. My parents were the last to go. I've been all alone since then. Nobody wants me, you see. Nobody cares no more."

She glanced more closely at the trumpet, saw that there was a possibility it could be repaired.

"You could play that instrument," she offered. "If you were as good as you say, you'd get gigs even now."

He scratched his dirt-streaked hair.

"Who would sit still and listen to a has-been or maybe some guy who never was?" he spoke, sighing forlornly. "Maybe all I ever did have was my stupidity in thinkin' that I was any good, you get what I'm sayin', lady?"

"I can help you," she insisted.

He coughed convulsively and Carla's heart went out to him.

"Sorry..." he told her as he caught his breath again and seemed to mean it. "What's some slick broad like you able to do for a godforsaken guy like me?"

"You think God has turned His back on you?"

"You blind or somethin'? I ain't seen nothing and no one showing me God's love lately."

"I am an entertainer myself. There are fifty thousand people inside this building who have paid to watch me."

"Oh..." he said, impressed but growing more uneasy. "Well, I'll be goin' now. You can't be late. Audiences hate that."

"I am very late already, mister," Carla remarked ruefully "A few more minutes could never matter."

She reached out for his arm.

"Let me take you inside," she said, understanding why he would hesitate, given his appearance and the body odors coming from him.

"I stink."

Carla had no need of being convinced of that.

"Yes, you do, mister, very badly," she agreed. "But a good shower can take care of that. And there are some stage clothes you can slip into. Would you tell me your name?"

"Thomas..." he blurted out, narrowed his eyes, the cynicism that was part of the outlook of most homeless people, especially the ones as bad off as he was, an instinctive fact of life that most of them never shed. "Thomas Gilboyne."

"God doesn't want you to end up like this, Thomas," she told him.

"And you speak for God, lady?" he asked. "Then ask Him to snuff me out like He does everybody else sooner or later."

Thomas coughed again, nearly collapsing to the ground and Carla thought for an instant that he was indeed dying, right before her eyes. She gripped his arm and held him upright, fighting her revulsion as she inhaled the rank odor of his body and filthy clothes.

As Carla glanced around desperately for help her silent prayer was answered when two stagehands appeared at the exit door. They stepped into the alley, both apparently about to light up cigarettes, since smoking was not permitted in most of the backstage area.

"Randy! Jeff!" Carla called out to them.

The young men ran over to her and she read the confusion on both faces as they took in the sight of Carla supporting the derelict musician. "Help me get him into the theater, please," she instructed. "He's sick. He needs a doctor."

"But Carla..." Randy began. He glanced nervously at the other stagehand.

"If you won't help, I'll do it myself," she insisted. She took a stumbling step forward doing her best to support the sick man and suddenly, Randy and Jeff moved to help her.

The company always traveled with a doctor and Carla knew her specific request to have Thomas examined and given the best possible medical care would not be ignored. He would in fact most likely get better medical attention here, she reflected, than in any of the city hospitals that would accept him as a patient.

The two stagehands gently carried Thomas Gilboyne between them, and as Carla opened the stage door, they took him inside.

He was beginning to regain consciousness, his bloodshot eyes widening.

"Am I where I think I am?" Thomas asked, casting a longing glance in the direction of the stage. "What did I do to deserve this?"

"You were God's instrument," she said, "and that makes you special."

"God used *me?*"

"He did, my new friend, he did use you in a wonderful way," Carla assured him as she smiled broadly.

Carla pointed out where the doctor's little office was.

"When you're finished," she said, "you can stay for my second performance."

"Second?" Tom repeated. "You must be bone tired after the first one."

"I do not *allow* myself that luxury!"

After they were done, Carla bowed her head for a moment.

"Lord, Lord, that could have been me a year ago or maybe a year from now," she prayed, "if You hadn't given my beloved Kyle to me. If only I could have done for him what he did for me."

She half expected the once persistent voice to say something but it did not, and she sensed that whoever it needed to help, it had been accomplished and now she was expected to take care of her part.

Carla cautiously stepped into the wings as she had done a thousand times over the years in hundreds of arenas but none as big as that one.

"Albert..." she whispered.

Perspiring heavily due to the strain of keeping the audience from bolting, Albert caught a glimpse of her.

Carla smiled, holding up one finger to show him that she needed just a minute, and he nodded in acknowledgment, then she hurried back to her dressing room, and prayed for a moment while holding her Bible tightly with both hands.

Then she headed back toward the wings. Albert saw that she was ready.

"And now, ladies and gentlemen," he announced, obviously relieved, his voice choking as tears mixed with sweat, "I am happy finally to present to you, tonight, the one and only Carla Gearhart."

The band immediately struck up its regular introductory music as the audience became absolutely quiet.

With some awkwardness in view of what had happened, Carla stepped out into the glare of spotlights.

"It's real amazing to me that you haven't left here by now," she confessed. "I would have, if I were sitting where you are."

A curly-haired young woman, dressed like a cowgirl in the front row, stood and smiled pleasantly as she said, "Carla, your friend told all of us what is going on in your life. We're waiting...because we love you. And our prayers go with you."

One by one, people were standing until nobody remained in their seat. In an instant, some fifty thousand pairs of hands started clapping, with a chorus of voices shouting, *"Carla, Carla, Carla!"*

Finally she signaled that she was ready to begin.

Visibly relieved, Albert handed her a cordless microphone and then left the stage but stayed in the wings, bowing his head as he prayed briefly.

"I remember a time when I would look out over an audience like this," Carla said, "and know that my beloved Kyle was sitting there among you, and I could sing my heart out to him. That made a big difference to me."

She paused, fighting back some fresh tears.

"But tonight I have only your love to reach out to," she added, "to sustain me, and that is all I need."

So it began that evening in Nashville, in an arena that had been completed only six months earlier, but no one would ever break her attendance over the ensuing years because no one had lived the drama that was hers and the man's to whom she would remain devoted through time and eternity.

"I believe in a God of miracles," she said, "and tonight is proof that He exists, that He cares, that He will be with us every step of the way, no matter how rebellious we are, no matter how many times we try His patience."

As Carla started to sing, memories came back in a flood that threatened to sweep her off the stage but she held on, as though that microphone were her life raft. She refused to do anything but sing from the center of her soul, sing of the love that had transformed her, love from Almighty God and, as well, from the wonderful man whom He had been gracious enough to send into her life.

"This first number is dedicated to Kyle Rivers," she said. "I guess my friend Albert told you a little of what's been going on. If only Kyle could feel tonight what you and I are experiencing."

...if only.

She had let "if onlys" rule her for far too long. It was time to declare her independence of them.

Carla started with her favorite gospel number, "He Lives." "'I serve a risen Saviour, He's in the world today. I know that He is living, whatever men may say.'"

Then she did something that not even her loyal band could have predicted.

"Lord..." she nearly whispered as she clipped the microphone to the front of her sequined dress.

The band members hesitated, trying to anticipate when Carla wanted them to join in again.

Her eyes sparkling, that resplendent hair like a crown of scarlet as it reflected the spotlights overhead, she thrust out her hands in front of her, palms upward, and spoke, "Dear Lord Jesus, take care of my beloved, for now, for eternity...."

And then the band, at a nod from her, started its accompaniment again.

"'I see His hand of mercy, I hear His voice of cheer,'" Carla Gearhart, eyes closed, continued singing words that had been written by someone else but were coming straight from her own heart and soul that night of nights in Nashville. "'And just the time I need Him he's always near. He lives, He lives...'"

No other song could have said it better.

Part One

Life has taught us that love does not consist in gazing at each other but in looking outward together in the same direction.

Saint-Exurpéry

Chapter One

Three months ago...

Carla had returned to Nashville from Hollywood after losing out on a movie role that she coveted, despite her Oscar win the year before. She was depressed, tempted to drown her sorrows in a bottle but with enough inner strength left to hold off just a bit longer.

Wandering the streets of Nashville, she recalled, *like some pitiable waif, depending upon the kindness of strangers.*

She had driven into town on her own, dismissing her driver, Rocco Gilardi, for the evening. The car she chose out of the half dozen she owned was her Jaguar convertible, driving it at top speed, the top down, the wind blowing her red hair in a dozen or more directions.

No state police stopped her, though she was hoping that someone would. She felt suicidal, wrenched as she was from the high of the Academy Awards triumph to being rejected in favor of a younger actress. Irving Chicolte had tried to argue that she was "big box office" now, her first picture after the Oscar earning $100 million plus in the United States alone where it played at a bit over two thousand theaters. Counting the foreign take, *Chasing Dreams* would eventually bring in nearly $200 million altogether, and that did not factor in the substantial video, cable and network broadcast revenue.

Yet she lost to someone ten years younger.

The news devastated her. Every time she passed by her Oscar statuette, it seemed to be mocking her, having promised a whole new world of career opportunities, and yet delivering little except invitations to entertainment industry functions which she had been attending anyway. Only now she was getting the better seats, either a table of her own or one that she would share on a given evening with the power elite.

From that glamorous company to the streets of Nashville, alone, walking aimlessly, not a soul in the world knowing or caring where I am tonight.

That was when she heard Kyle's voice.

She stopped short, listening.

He left the splendor of heaven, knowing His destiny was the lonely hill of Golgotha, there to lay down His life for me....

She could not move, could not open her mouth or shut her eyes or turn her head.

If that isn't love, the ocean is dry, there's no star in the sky, and the sparrow can't fly!

Suddenly she seemed to be gasping, as though someone had placed a pillow over her face and was suffocating her.

If that isn't love, then heaven's a myth, there's no feeling like this, if that isn't love.

A brief pause.

Then the second stanza was being sung.

Two voices.

She realized that there were two voices, one of which

was strangely familiar, the other not recognizable at all. But it was the second that had hooked her, that had grabbed hold of her body and was now tugging at it.

Finally she could move.

She walked slowly, still unaware of her surroundings, her senses locked in on that voice as though it were a radar signal, drawing her toward it.

Lights ahead. Flashing lights.

Above the entrance to one of the myriad little clubs that was part of the Nashville music scene, clubs where fledgling country music stars often got their first taste of performing in public.

She walked up to the front door, which was open, and went inside.

In an instant she recognized one of the two performers on stage.

Darcy Reuther.

Carla had known the woman for many years.

What are you doing in a club like this? she thought. You're a star. You should never descend back to this level. Are you crazy?

But then her attention drifted to the man standing next to Darcy. He was about a foot taller than she, dressed in jeans and a white T-shirt and black vest.

As they finished the song, the audience of a few dozen people burst into applause that was loud and sustained. But nothing took Carla's attention away from Darcy Reuther's singing partner.

"I wrote that before Kyle Rivers was born," Darcy said after the room was quieter, "so I guess I'm *old enough to be his grandmother!*"

Laughter.

"But I'm not that fortunate," she continued. "Nothing would have made me happier than to say Kyle is my grandson. I would have been very proud of him, as a young man, as a young singer.''

She turned to him.

"Kyle, would you do that number we discussed?" she asked.

He smiled, and nodded, then turned to the band leader and asked him to cease any accompaniment.

That departure from the norm for such clubs had not been scripted, so the members of the band seemed confused.

"I feel a special leading tonight," he said. "All I need is my guitar."

The band leader nodded understandingly, and gave him the sign of the cross.

"Praise God, brother, and thank you," Kyle said.

And he began to sing "Amazing Grace" as Carla had never heard it sung before. Carla found herself staring at him, hardly blinking.

On the final stanza, Darcy Reuther joined in with Kyle.

"'When we've been there ten thousand years, bright shining as the sun,''' they sang as though they had been doing duets together for a very long time, "'we've no less days to sing God's praise than when we'd first begun.'"

Carla could not move, not even to join in with the applause.

And then Darcy Reuther noticed that she was in the audience.

"We have a special patron tonight," she said, "someone who is a country music legend and, now, an Oscar-winning actress."

She pointed in Carla's direction.

"Carla Gearhart is here tonight. Won't you come up on-stage, my dear friend?"

She did not want to do anything but leave, but she was

caught literally in the spotlight and, in order to be gracious, she had to accept Darcy's invitation.

After having met many male performers during ten years as a singer, while she was making hundreds of appearances in the main metropolitan areas of the United States as well as small country locations, Carla should not have been nervous to stand next to Kyle, to have him whisper into her ear that he had been a fan for a long time, to look briefly into his eyes.

"Carla, you didn't really plan on this," Darcy Reuther observed, "so I can't ask you to sing anything tonight."

As she said that, everyone in the small audience seemed to start shouting, "Sing, Carla, sing!"

She was at her best when she had had plenty of time to rehearse and so the idea of singing with no preparation played havoc with her normal confidence on stage.

"I have no idea what I could do tonight," she muttered, partly to the audience, partly to Darcy.

Kyle whispered, "What about 'Were You There?' You sing the first stanza. I'll do the second. Darcy can take the third. And the three of us can sing the fourth together."

As an afterthought, he asked, "Do you know it?"

"Yes…I do," she told him nervously.

"Let's go ahead then, okay?"

"Sure."

He kissed her on the cheek.

Carla had not sung that hymn in years but, somehow, she had never forgotten the words, the tempo, anything about it.

"'Were you there when they crucified my Lord?'" she began. "'Were you there when they crucified my Lord? Sometimes it causes me to tremble, tremble, tremble.'"

And she felt better about her unexpected performance in that little club than others that she had spent long hours rehearsing in order to face tens of thousands of people in a single stadium or arena.

Kyle and Darcy could do nothing but stand amazed, Carla seemingly at the top of her form during those few minutes.

Now it was Kyle's turn.

"'When through the woods and forest glades I wander, and hear the birds sing sweetly in the trees...'" he sang with great skill, imbuing that less familiar stanza with a power that seemed to shake the ceiling and the walls of the club.

Next, Darcy stepped into the spotlight.

"Something special is happening tonight," she said. "I have heard the greatest female voice in the history of country-and-western, and I have heard the greatest young man's voice in ages, and I must step aside. The spotlight is theirs tonight."

More applause, louder, sustained.

"I have to ask Carla Gearhart and Kyle Rivers to sing the remaining stanzas while I sit down and enjoy them as you all are doing," Darcy continued. "This is not a church, this club, but that's okay, for I feel the Holy Spirit here just the same, and I think He is saying, *'Let Carla and Kyle be a blessing to everyone!'*"

The next day, Carla and Kyle went on their first date, beginning a relationship that they would come to pray would last a lifetime, and beyond.

Chapter Two

Carla had never met anyone like Kyle before.

The men she had known were veterans of show business and life itself. She could never think of them in the same way as she was beginning to think of Kyle.

Strong…

He was strong physically, but there was a strength of the spirit that she found appealing as well, which did not translate into arrogance.

She talked with him about this during their fourth date, a simple one that involved dinner, a movie and a walk through one of Nashville's parks.

"You are just so solid," she told him.

"I work out a lot," he replied.

Chuckling, Carla said, "That much is obvious."

They were holding hands as they walked, enjoying the cool evening after an especially humid day.

"It's something else," she explained.

"Tell me…" he encouraged her, pointing to a bench where they could sit down.

"I have known men who never seemed to look me

straight in the eye. You could tell that their minds were someplace else or that they felt insecure."

"Or, maybe, it seemed that they were always planning something, always thinking of an angle."

"That's about it, Kyle. How did you know?"

This was one aspect of his personality that Carla had not decided whether she liked or hated. He seemed prone to honest answers at any given moment. She could not help wondering how much of what he told her along such lines was not wisdom but simple judgments that were inherently superficial.

But this time he had a good reason to say what he did.

"I've dated some women who were the same type," he told her. "Pretty infuriating at times."

"Is *calculating* a better word?" Carla ventured.

"Well, yes. There was no way I could trust them."

"How about me?" she asked.

He sucked in his breath as he exclaimed, "Oh, brother!" then looked rather sheepish seconds later.

"Is it that bad?" Carla asked.

"It isn't. But you aren't perfect."

She had never had any illusions. If anything, she tended to dwell too much on her imperfections.

"That's funny," Carla remarked.

"What's funny?" Kyle asked defensively, unsure of whether she was making fun of him or not.

"You...."

Jumping to conclusions, he was beginning to feel rather awkward and uncomfortable just then. "What's funny about me?" he asked.

"I kind of think that you're perfect, Kyle."

"No!" he declared, his insecurity gone but something of even more concern replacing it. "I'm not. Only one man was."

"Jesus?"

"Yes, Jesus. He was the only truly perfect man. The Bible says so, and I have never felt otherwise."

"What about me? Is there something that I have a tendency to do that annoys you, Kyle?"

"Nothing, really."

"But you said I wasn't perfect."

"You seem edgy now."

"Edgy? What do you mean?"

"As though you're waiting."

She was now the one to face insecurity, regretting that she had ever gone in the direction of what the two of them were discussing.

"You've lost me," Carla spoke.

"Waiting for me to let you down."

She was silent for a moment, then nodded grudgingly.

"So it's true!" Kyle exclaimed, surprised at himself.

"Yes, it is," Carla admitted.

"You must have been hurt real bad in the past."

"I have been."

"You think I'm too good to be true, is that it?"

"Pretty much."

"I'm real, Carla. I don't have time for subterfuge, you know. The games that people play with one another...I hate that sort of thing. I live life with more urgency than a lot of people because none of us know what tomorrow will bring."

"So do I. But it seems to be all that I have ever known. Few quiet moments, not much occasion to trust in the Lord, as you would say."

"How sad."

"Oh, yes, *sad* is the right word."

"Not knowing who to trust—what that must do to your emotions!"

"But it's typical of my profession. Phoniness is common. And actors are good at this, good at being convincing.

They rope you in, and then when they are through with you, they cast you aside.''

"Have *you* done that to others?" Kyle asked.

She looked at him, having hoped that he would not ask her anything like that but now that he had, she struggled with an answer.

"I have," she acknowledged. "There have been relationships built on pretense and deceit."

"Is the one between us any different, Carla?"

"Of course."

"You say that easily."

"I meant it. I think that I am—"

She stopped herself.

"Go ahead," he encouraged her.

"It's hard," she said.

"Hard to be honest?"

"Very hard, Kyle."

"I'm willing to listen. I won't pull away, Carla. I'll stay right here and you can tell me whatever it is that you want to say."

"Falling in love with you," she said, forcing the words out.

He smiled in his most sensual way.

"I've got something to tell you," he said, his voice not much above a whisper.

His gaze did not waver. She felt as though he were looking right into the center of her soul.

"Carla, it's the same with me," he finally told her. "I think I'm beginning to fall in love with you."

Part of her rejoiced at hearing him say that but another part did not, the part that had felt so much hurt over the years, so much disappointment in her relationships with men.

"You don't know what you're getting into," she admitted.

"I think I do."

"You can't possibly know!"

"You're an actress. What more is there?"

"I've not been as pure in my life as you have."

"Do you think I'm naive, Carla? I have friends who have been in show business for many years. I know what goes on."

"I've not been as bad as some women I know. My involvements...never with married men. I—"

"Shush!" he told her. "None of that matters."

"If you only knew!"

"I don't *need* to know."

"But—"

"But *nothing*, Carla! Last week, you and I went to church. And you walked down the center aisle when the invitation was given at the conclusion of the service."

It had been a remarkable experience for her. She seemed to have been lifted up out of her seat and nearly pushed down the aisle.

"The sermon seemed to be about people like me," she recalled.

"I think it was, Carla...about people who are convinced that they have led a life so sinful that there can never be forgiveness for them, not ever, as though God has written them off. Do you feel the same way now?"

She felt some resentment at how he was categorizing her feelings but not enough to contradict him, at least not then.

"Not as much. But you can't expect me to change in an instant."

"That's right, I can't. Yet I want you to know *right now* that since God has forgiven you, and forgotten your sins, so have I. As far as He is concerned, they never occurred. They are gone, totally, eternally gone. It's that way with me as well, Carla."

"Are you sure?" she pressed. "Are you absolutely sure, Kyle?"

"As sure as I am of my Lord Himself."

He reached out for her, and she moved a few inches into the circle of his arms.

"It's as though I have never lived before now," she whispered, hating to feel so emotionally naked at that relatively early stage of their relationship, but unable to restrain herself, unable to slip into some kind of deception.

"The difference is that you now have something really worth living for," he told her. "It makes all the difference in the world."

She wanted to dispute this young man named Kyle Rivers, to tell him how close to arrogance that statement was, but she stopped herself, because she realized that he was not talking wholly about himself but, rather, Someone else.

"I do...." she continued whispering.

"You do what?" he asked.

"I do love you."

She smiled at him.

"I want to kiss you now," Carla said, "the longest, sweetest kiss in history!"

"You expect me to object to that?"

"Not one bit."

"Well, I don't."

...the longest, sweetest kiss in history.

It probably did not come close to achieving that record but *trying* was still a lot of fun.

Chapter Three

Another side of Kyle that Carla saw was his exceptional thoughtfulness, which never seemed put on but to come from the center of his soul....

Her parents both had had to be confined to a retirement center months before she won her Oscar, and so they couldn't be in the audience at the ceremonies that night. She had arranged for a videotape of the ceremonies and a few days later visited her parents at the center, but Alzheimer's disease's relentless march had speeded up a bit, and no one could be certain how much her mother understood about what was going on around her. As for her father, caring for his beloved had proved too demanding, bringing on him a stroke that left most of his body paralyzed.

Kyle and she had visited them for the first time just two weeks ago, and Carla would never forget what one of the nurses had told her.

"Treat him good!" the heavyset woman whispered to her while Kyle was in the men's room.

"Kyle?" Carla replied. "I wouldn't do otherwise."

"He's a treasure."

"How do you mean?"

"It's something like when we bring in animals now and then."

"What do you mean?"

"There is a bond that develops almost immediately, it never seems to fail. Cats especially are a real blessing to these people, you know. Something in a cat, a sensitivity that is just beautiful to witness. The elderly, even the ones worst off, seem to come out of some kind of inner world for the few minutes that they can hold those warm, purring bodies."

"What does this have to do with Kyle?"

"It's in him, too, that ability to connect with people. I've never seen anything like that. What a doctor he would make! This friend of yours is special. I've watched him. He seems to ease the pain of anyone whose hand he holds. I think he does repair their emotions. This lasts only as long as he is with me, but, then, it may be a continuous process, and this is just an awfully important first step."

The nurse stopped speaking. Smiling, she added, "What it must be like to have him hold you in his arms. He must be a passionate man."

Carla agreed that he was.

"You are real lucky," the nurse remarked.

"It's not luck," Carla told her honestly. "It's God opening up his heart and mine to one another."

"But you might never have met him. That's luck, the fact that you did, right?"

"No, it isn't. It's pure and simple—an answer to a prayer for Kyle and for me. I was lonely. So was he. We felt that way before we ever met one another."

The nurse nodded as she smiled strangely, and then went about her duties elsewhere in the center.

Carla had lost track of Kyle, but assumed he would be with her parents.

She was right.

He was kneeling in front of her mother's wheelchair.

Normally, looking impossibly thin-faced, frail, not much more than a living skeleton, Rosemary Gearhart would not have been able to pay any attention to him or anyone else unless she was in a comparatively and increasingly rare lucid moment, but there was no way to predict when this would happen.

But, for Kyle, it would prove different. Every time he subsequently visited her, she would react like she did on that first occasion.

As Carla stood in the doorway, her mother was reaching up to touch Kyle's smooth cheek.

"Where's the beard?" she said.

He chuckled agreeably as he told her, "I just don't have a coarse beard, ma'am."

Her fingers touched his strong chin.

"Nice," she said knowingly.

Kyle was surprised at the way she talked, and delighted that she was responding as well as she did.

"Why, thank you, Miss Gearhart!" he told her.

She touched his lips next.

"Are you a good kisser?" she asked abruptly.

"I don't know how to answer that."

Carla saw a chance to enter the little tableau.

"He is a *very* good kisser, Mother," she said, smiling broadly, while Kyle blushed a very deep red.

Her mother looked up at her and, then, in an instant, the blankness that was part of Alzheimer's returned, as though her comprehension, to the extent that she could grasp anything at all, was now trained on a scene beyond that one, a scene that only she could visualize.

That would not be Kyle's only visit.

Over the coming weeks, he would return to the center

half a dozen times. Carla did not have to ask him to join her.

"Are you going to visit your folks this evening?" he would say.

"Yes, I am," she replied. "You've got my schedule down pat, don't you?"

"Of course."

During the other visits, Kyle seemed to be in demand all over the center, with an astonishing number of requests for a little of his time before he left. Gradually the visits began to last longer.

Carla could not have been more pleased because she was privileged to witness another side of Kyle's personality that only confirmed what she felt about him.

She would never forget what he told her on the way back to her house that first time, after she asked him about her mother and the other residents at the center.

"What was it like?" she spoke.

"Strange at first," he said.

"How do you mean strange?"

"I am usually a little shy being that close to strangers. Onstage, it's not difficult for me at all. The audience is a sea of faces and they all blend together."

"You can say that again!" Carla echoed his reaction.

"After all, I am not one-on-one with any of them. But today, I must have spent time with at least a dozen folks, aging men and women who needed me a lot more than anyone in any audience has."

"At the start, it was awkward for you back there."

"It's the shyness I mentioned. But that passed soon enough."

"I'm really sorry that I subjected you to all that, Kyle, and without much warning."

"Oh, no, Carla, it was fine. I was enjoying myself but then, at some point, it went beyond ordinary enjoyment."

"And became—" Carla prompted him.

He paused, recalling how he felt, the expressions on pale, wrinkled, liver-mark-splotched faces.

"I thought of what it would be like when my own parents reach that stage in their lives," he said. "Could I help them in some way also?"

"You were saying that the way you felt went beyond carnal enjoyment as such."

Kyle leaned over and kissed the tip of her nose.

"Something spiritual," he said, "my soul touching theirs."

She rubbed her arm.

"That sounds wonderful but—"

"Eerie?"

"Exactly the word I would have used!"

"I agree with you. But it was pure and beautiful, not dark and sinister, Carla. God's purpose was being fulfilled."

...God's purpose was being fulfilled.

"I need to learn a great deal. I don't have the fix on His Will that you seemed to be blessed with, Kyle."

"But you can learn. That's the wonderful thing about faith. It can only grow, and along with that growth comes experience."

He was holding her hand in one of his own.

"Some are willing and will learn nothing," he told her. "Those who are *eager* to learn will be given much."

"Kyle?" she asked.

"Yes, my love?" he replied with such warmth that she wanted to hold him so tightly that their hearts would be practically touching one another, making it difficult for Carla to control her emotions.

"I have one criticism," she said, gulping a couple of times.

Kyle was frowning as he asked, "Criticism of—?"

Carla had not meant to make him nervous in any way but that was how he seemed to be reacting.

"You, Kyle."

"Me?"

He looked so good, his bright blond hair glistening as a ray of sunlight framed the top of his head.

"A halo," she muttered, trying to get out of the corner into which she had backed herself. "You've actually got a halo around your—"

"You're changing the subject, Carla."

"I guess I am."

He was teasing her a bit but with an edge of seriousness as well and said, "You were about to tell me what that one criticism is."

"I guess I was."

"What is it? No more evasion, okay?"

"Okay," she told him.

"Well?"

Carla hesitated, not sure when or if she should say anything after all.

"Go ahead...." Kyle kept prodding. "There is not one word or a thousand in the English language that you would use that could ever offend me or make me want to reconsider our relationship, okay, Carla?"

She was grateful for that reassurance.

"You are beginning to sound like some ultrasophisticated whoever from New York City or someplace. It's almost like you are putting on a facade that you hope people will think is real. You weren't like that when we first met. You sounded much more—"

"—normal?" he finished the sentence for her.

"Well, yes, that's right."

"You're not the only one to point that out to me. My father said something just a few days ago."

Kyle pulled the car over to the side of the road.

"Carla," he said earnestly, "I've dated lots of women, you know. I think each one was special in her own way. But you're different. You are very special. I find that I am always stretching myself emotionally to keep up with you."

"But I don't understand why you would feel that way. We're on the same level. I've never felt that I was above you."

He seemed unconvinced.

"I want to be a proper husband, a man you can respect. Rely on. I don't know all that much about you yet I know enough to say that I am looking forward to us spending the rest of our lives together. And I don't want you to be ashamed of me when we meet those big-time executives you know. It would be terrible for your career to have people saying that you settled for me out of wild passion, that there was no real love involved. What if important folks started whispering, 'He might be a good lover but he doesn't have a brain in his head.'"

Kyle cupped her head in his hands.

"And I want to think that I can be a proper father to any children the Lord blesses us with, Carla, that they can be proud of me, too."

Listening to Kyle talk about their future, about marriage and the children they would raise together someday, Carla felt so moved with love she couldn't speak. She took his hand, threading her fingers through his. Staring down at their hands clasped together, she spoke in a quiet voice, one straight from her heart.

"I respect you more than any man I have ever known. More than anyone rich, or powerful or famous. I am proud to be with you and the proudest day of my life will be the day I become your wife." She smiled tenderly at him. "I hope we'll be blessed with children. And I pray I'll be a good mother. I thought I'd done it all and knew it all when

I met you. But now I know there's still a lot I have to learn about life and about relationships, too.''

He slipped his arm around her shoulders and pulled her close. "We have a lifetime ahead of us, my love. To discover it all together.''

Chapter Four

An Oscar!

It was coveted by virtually everyone in the moviemaking business.

Carla Gearhart had placed the statuette on the mantel over her fireplace at her home in Brentwood, Tennessee almost as a talisman to ward off failure.

For a while it seemed to be working. Winning an Academy Award for Best Actress had opened up a new career for her and revived the one she had started with when she was in her late teens: country music.

What a night that Monday was, with an in-person attendance of thirty-five hundred producers, directors, studio executives and many others, as well as a television viewing audience numbering into the millions.

Betting handicappers in Las Vegas and elsewhere were loading the odds against her, in part because no country music singer had ever gone from the Grand Ole Opry to any kind of real movie stardom, but also due to the kind of role that she had played: an obsessive, control freak mother who drove her daughter to a successful suicide attempt and her husband to booze. The film was dark, sad, largely downbeat. And her competition included more than one previous Academy Award winner.

Yet she won.

Columnists, media reviewers and others speculated after the ceremony had ended that Carla had been absolutely convincing in playing a character who was utterly opposite her own personality. None of the others did anything that the Academy Award voter had not seen them do before, however well they did it.

Carla was a breath of fresh air!

The morning after the annual ceremony in Hollywood, and the winners' parties afterward, was precisely when her agent received a dozen phone calls from the various studios as well as major independent producers, most of whom would have little to do with her before she was able to hold the Oscar in her hand, and smile.

"You've got no worries, Carla!" Irving Chicolte had told her over lunch that next day, less than two hours after she had managed to drag herself out of bed, the two of them now sitting at a favored table in the most coveted section of a restaurant only minutes from the auditorium. But then Irving was a master of feel-good sensibilities, and would have told her the same thing if she had just been signed to do a role in a grade C quickie.

He was a genuinely sweet man, this bald-headed, bushy eye-browed, dimpled little character, a leftover from another era, surviving, and doing it well, in an industry of cookie-cutter young Turks, some of the other agents laughing at flashy old Irving behind his back but, at the same time, jealous of the deals he was able to secure for his clients, some of whom had been with him for decades.

More honest than he was willing to admit for fear of blowing his image, Irving Chicolte turned down deals that were suspect, telling people that he could not face his cigar in the morning if he ever threw his integrity out the window. Producers and studio executives, while not themselves above shady business from time to time, found dealing with Irving curiously reassuring, which was why he still had a varied roster of clients.

But it was Carla Gearhart who invariably seemed to require a wholly disproportionate percentage of the man's efforts. She was hardly over the hill, but her singing career *had* been sliding because she revealed a penchant for accepting *any* kind of gig anywhere just to keep working. The only time she truly felt alive and functioning as a worthwhile human being was onstage before an audience. Her act defined her as a woman, because her work was her only reason for living.

Until *Promises*.

The truth got through even to Carla eventually.

Irving received the script from a producer at a major Burbank film studio who had her in mind for a part other than the lead. But as Irving read it, he had some sort of hunch that she was just right for that main role. He campaigned for the change, telling the producer and the studio brass bankrolling *Promises* that they could not have her for any part *except* the starring one. And Irving was promptly told that this was a possibility but she would have to screen-test for it. Irving assured them that this was fine.

His hand was shaking as he hung up the phone on his cherry wood desk in an office that was more like a plush penthouse suite.

What have I done? he thought. *I must have let the pressure rot my brain. It can't be anything else.*

Two nightmares.

One that he would have to face was telling Carla about the screen test; the other was getting her to do something better than simply coast through it on the assumption that being a big name in one sector of the entertainment world made her automatically an equivalent powerhouse in another.

Irving thought he would have to battle her for days.

But when he asked Carla, she agreed right away. Not one second of hesitation! And she rehearsed like a woman possessed, almost maniacal in her determination.

The result: she got the role, and just over a year and a month later, won an Oscar for best starring role as an actress.

Finally, at lunch the following day, Irving managed enough chutzpah to ask her why she gave him no trouble when he told her about *Promises* originally.

"That surprised me, too," she confessed.

"What are you saying?" he asked, puzzled. "That you don't *know* why you went along easily?"

Her smile then was the most radiant he had seen for a very long time.

"Obviously something is going on here," Irving observed slyly.

"As I look back now," Carla said, "I guess I can think of a reason that I wasn't aware of at the time."

"Tell me, Carla."

"Because it was what God wanted. There's a verse in the New Testament that suggests God gives each of us who acknowledge our dependence on Him a certain peace that passes understanding from time to time."

"God?" Irving repeated. "New Testament? Carla, you're scaring me." Carla knew Irving had been raised a Christian but his faith had long ago lapsed.

"Yes, God, my good friend. And not like that cigar-smoking old comic actor, either."

"I never heard you talk about Him before now."

She paused, thinking, and then threw her head back, long strands of flame red hair flowing down her back, and said, "I have met a man."

"So what does that have to do with God?" Irving asked lamely.

"Because, I think, it's true that heaven opened up and dropped Kyle Rivers right in my lap."

Irving Chicolte was twenty-five years older than Carla, and looked it, while she was in her early thirties and could have played a high school or college student.

"Now, now, I feel happy for you," he told her, the father part of him coming to the surface. "But I've got to ask why you have kept him a secret until today?"

"I wanted to make sure that there was something serious going on. I didn't want to find myself hooked by his looks or his charm only to find that's all it was."

"Fair enough, Carla. Now my second question: How long have you known him?"

"Only a few weeks."

He was astonished, theatrically slamming the palm of his hand down on the round wood table.

"And already he is God's gift?"

Next, he threw his hands up in gesture of disbelief, a reaction he'd perfected over the years. Learning such gestures, especially in Hollywood, had served him well over the years.

"I've never met him. What's the problem?"

"He lives in Nashville."

"Is that all, Carla?" Irving asked, knowing all too well when she was being less than totally forthcoming.

Carla blushed as she admitted, "You got me again."

Irving's eyes narrowed.

"Come out with it," he insisted. "I need to know."

"Kyle's gotten involved in church activities."

Irving was surprised but took that in stride.

"The rest of it, my dear," he probed. "I don't condemn men who spend time in church instead of bars."

Carla wanted to spit the words out right away instead of

hesitating but she equivocated a bit until Irving demanded
that she let everything out once and for all.

"And there are his college classes," she said. "These
take all morning and most of the afternoon."

That one got through big-time!

Irving had been sipping from a glass of white wine, and
was so startled that he spilled half of it on the table.

"Are you—?" he asked hopefully but with an increasing
edge of chilling resignation, knowing his client nearly as
well as he had his ex-wives.

Carla nodded.

"Yes, Irving, I *am* serious," she said. "I will never de-
ceive you or play some odd practical joke."

"Tell me that, at least, he's a senior. *Please* tell me that,
my dear."

"I can't."

She reached out, placed her right hand on the back of
his left.

"He's a music teacher at college...." she said rather
sheepishly.

"Holy Mother of—!" he started to shout but stopped
when he saw a monsignor, who was sitting at the next table,
turn around and glare at him.

For a moment Irving was quiet, and Carla knew why.
He was already planning what might be called damage control.

"I can imagine what the tabloids will do with this
if...*when* they find out," he said, an old stutter long ago
conquered threatening to resurrect itself. "But then, if you
never see him again, the chances are—"

Carla knew the routine, knew the kind of pressures Irving
was going to put on her so that she would cave in and do
what he wanted.

"I will *not* stop seeing Kyle," she said firmly but without raising her voice.

"Is he that good in bed, Carla?"

She might have slapped anybody else who would talk to her like that but she knew Irving Chicolte as well as he knew her, and she had come to accept such outspokenness as evidence of his honesty, even if it said a great deal about his lack of taste.

"We've not *been* together that way," she said.

"Soon, I'm sure," he muttered.

"No, Irving, now stop it!"

He cleared his throat and added, "But, dear, dear Carla, that's what *everyone* will be saying. You're deceiving your-self if you think otherwise. At this point in your career, do you want people suspecting that you are running around with a college kid? It might send the message that you couldn't get anybody your own age."

Carla knew that Irving would not beat around the bush when she told him. And she was prepared.

"He teaches at a college, Irving. He's not a student," Carla replied patiently. "There's something else," she added.

"Not again!" he exclaimed. "You're going to tell me that he's got a prison record, but you love him despite everything."

"Irving..." she tried to say.

"How can I ever explain this to our friends, let alone our enemies, of which there are a few in this town?"

"Irving, please!"

"Don't you realize what is happening to your career now that you are an Academy Award winner?"

Carla reached out and put the palm of her hand over his mouth.

"Irving, *enough!*"

He quieted down.

"Any *more* surprises?" he asked, fully expecting that she might have a few more up her sleeve.

"He's younger than me, yes. But not all that much. And he's gorgeous," she said, "and the absolute best male country music singer I have ever heard. I want you to meet Kyle Rivers, and see if you agree that he could be very big."

"Is it love, Carla," Irving asked cynically, "or a career opportunity?"

She had been all in favor of her agent's renowned outspokenness until he said that.

"If I didn't find you so adorable," she said, "I'd fire you right now."

"If I didn't think of you with so much affection," he told her, "I would go without protest, sighing with relief all the way to my attorney's office, my dear."

"So, will you go?"

"To Nashville?"

"Yes, Nashville."

He shrugged his shoulders.

"With less than the greatest anticipation."

"Why do you say that, Irving? I've not seen quite this attitude coming from you before now."

"I think, in your present state, you would find a hog caller good enough to audition for the Metropolitan Opera!"

He smiled at her, then added, "Will I like this Kyle Rivers, Carla? I mean, really like him?"

"You will find him charming *and* talented."

"Is it love, Carla? Can you be sure? I couldn't bear to see you hurt."

Carla smiled softly, her eyes shining. He had his answer.

Car horns were honking.

"We're blocking the driveway," she said. "Let's go, Irving."

He half smiled, nodded and drove away.

"I'll ask my secretary to make the travel arrangements,"

Irving said as they approached his office where one of her own cars was parked in the building's garage.

"The Opryland Hotel would be fine."

"When should we plan on going?"

"This is Monday. How about leaving on Thursday?"

"Roxie and I could make it earlier, if you want."

"Okay, Wednesday would be fine."

He was getting out of the car when Carla reached over and grabbed his sleeve.

"Irving?" she asked.

"Yes, Carla?" he said, sounding a bit weary.

"Can I tell Kyle when I call him later?"

"About us coming? That would be fine."

"No, about your prayer need."

He hesitated, then acknowledged, "I haven't had a Christian offer to pray for me or my loved ones lately."

"I *am* now a professing Christian, Irving."

"For how long?"

"Just a few weeks."

"You might get over it soon then."

"I'm sorry you feel that way," she said sincerely.

He kissed her on the cheek, then got out of his car and walked up the sloping driveway to the pavement outside. His shoulders were slumped, his walk shuffling.

"Irving!" she shouted. "I love you!"

"Yeah, yeah," he replied, waving back at her, and then was gone from sight, swallowed up by the glare of the sun as he emerged from the relative darkness of the garage, an aging veteran of the Hollywood entertainment world, able to make the most arrogant stars and studio executives dread his ire but now tired of going to "war" every day and being so wired at night that a restful sleep is something he cherished almost as much as life itself.

Carla called Kyle as soon as she was inside her apartment, which was more like a miniature mansion, with black

Italian marble floors, white imported furniture and a large crystal chandelier.

"Did you go and tell Irving that you and I were getting married?" he asked.

She knew that Kyle, always a model of directness, would ask that very question.

"I didn't have the nerve frankly," Carla replied honestly.

"He's been so much a part of your life for so long. Shouldn't you avoid giving him any surprises?"

Carla had been asking herself that same question.

"I want him to meet you first," she said a bit defensively.

"If that's what you think is best."

Not again! her mind shouted. *You keep doing that.*

Again and again...sometimes when Kyle was acquiescing too readily, it seemed as though this indicated weakness on his part, or that he was afraid of losing her if he disagreed about anything. She had never found indecisive yes-men very attractive for long.

"I wish you would stop that," she told him at last.

"What, Carla? Stop what?"

"Always giving in to me. You really can disagree with what I say, you know, and it won't mean that we are going to split up."

"I know that."

As always, his voice disarmed her. The first time they spoke weeks before, and during that conversation, the circumstances were not any different. Kyle's deep, warm voice had an amazing effect on her. It was not harsh at all, as though coming from some macho football hero whose vocal cords had been affected by chewing tobacco and booze, but, rather, an inexpressibly sexy one that seemed almost like a caressing hand. But she was determined not to let it detour her from finding out what she wanted.

"Then why did you leave it up to me again?" she asked, trying very hard not to sound peevish.

Carla knew how much she was gambling by confronting him just then.

"Irving is your agent, your friend, has been for all these years," he stated. "How can I help you with a man I've not even met?"

That made sense but the same voice she loved to hear was also one that showed naked emotion, making it easy for her to read, and so she asked, "Is there something more, though, Kyle, now if not other times?"

"Yes, there is. Maybe I am afraid of losing you. It wouldn't be the first time I've lost someone I loved," he admitted.

"Tell me."

"I thought I loved a girl about nine years ago. We were both still in high school."

Somehow that was hardly a shocking revelation as far as Carla was concerned, especially from a man with Kyle's assets.

"At the beginning, I was real surprised that Christie Nugent would want to have anything to do with me," he added without a trace of guile.

Carla wondered what the other guys in his high school were like!

"But then I lost her," he continued, his voice not much above a whisper.

"The two of you split?"

"No, Carla. She was killed in an automobile accident."

"Sorry..."

"That's all right. After all, you don't know *everything* about me."

She waited for Kyle to continue, not wanting to force out of him what must have been unbearably painful at the time and later.

"She was just over six feet tall, a Nashville beauty queen. I was three inches shorter. People joked about the two of us, Mutt and Jeff, you know. She wanted to be a model. In fact, the top agent at the time was interested in her, met with Christie on a stopover from New York City. You'd have to be completely blind not to see that this agent thought she could make it big."

"So Christie was all set?" she spoke.

"Yes. Ready for the big time." He paused. "And then it happened, just five minutes after school one afternoon. Another student, who had stayed away that day, was on drugs. He went past a stop sign. Christie had one of those small two-seater English sports cars, almost as old as she was. And the guy was driving his father's lumbering four-door sedan."

Kyle cut himself off for a bit, and she could tell that he was fighting to control his emotions.

"Let's not talk about this anymore," Carla told him, trying to change the subject for his sake.

"What happened hit hard, but then it was over, and, yeah, I spent months in grief, but I learned to go on, despite some baggage."

"Losing people you love?"

"Yes..."

Then, as often before, Carla could almost feel that she happened to be the one who needed to learn a great deal about life.

Chapter Five

During the flight, while Irving was sound asleep, Roxie told Carla of her militant atheism, which she had come to as a result of the tragedy in her life, declaring that the concept of God is for fools....

The plane arrived late due to heavier air traffic than usual over Nashville, circling for an hour before it landed, and taking the better part of another half hour before it was pulled into its gate.

"I had hoped to get you both some time with Kyle before he performs," Carla told them as they were waiting for their luggage. "But the delay means we'll just be able to get to my house, and freshen up a bit before we head off for the college."

"It's not a professional gig," Roxie said snootily, "so why the rush? He can go on late if he wants. Even the pros do that these days. The fans will always be there, whatever happens."

"Is that the way to think of the people who have given your husband and I a wonderful living for so long now?"

"You're right," the other woman relented. "I don't normally think or talk that way."

"About Kyle's gig tonight?"

"Yes?"

"It really is a professional one," Carla told her. "People are paying good money to see him. Several record label reps have assured us that they will be there."

"But you can't count on what any of them say. They've been known to talk out of both sides of their mouths."

Rocco Gilardi, a former nightclub bouncer, guided the limo in the direction of the house where Carla had lived for more than a decade, a very large estate that some in the country music world suggested was the grandest residence they had ever seen, eclipsing anything that Kenny, Johnny, Hank or any of the other greats had had over at the height of their stardom.

Roxie was stunned.

"I never dreamed you've been living like this," she admitted. "I mean, Rusty Reynolds earned more than $21 million last year but she doesn't have anything like this."

Irving spoke up.

"Remember that Dwayne pulled in over $33 million, and *his* house looks like some fixer-upper compared to these digs," he said, though he had seen it several times since it was built five years earlier.

But then, none of those other stars had won an Academy Award.

Set behind a gold-and-black gate, right in the midst of fifteen acres of well-tended grounds, the house had three floors, and a five column front porch reached by driving up a winding driveway bordered by Italian cypress trees that were twenty feet tall.

Even Roxie's mouth was hanging open as they pulled up to the front electrically controlled gate.

"It's not quite as private as it looks," Carla acknowledged. "Reporters with one-thousand millimeter telephoto lenses can see right up to and partway into the house."

"Close the drapes," Roxie offered flippantly. "That's simple enough, isn't it?"

"Not like you would assume, my dear," Carla retorted. "There are twenty windows in the front of the house, and thirty more along the side and across the back. It would be quite a job opening and closing them several times each day."

Roxie was never one to easily relinquish the last word, and said, "Keep them closed then."

"I wouldn't get natural light," Carla told her. "And I want to be able to look out at my property without having to part drapes each time."

"You're too young to be so set in your ways."

"I see. Well, then, what advantage does age bring you, Roxie?"

"The ability to know when something is nonsense or not."

The intent of that remark was hardly subtle.

"We're back to my faith then," Carla said.

"I am not criticizing you, Carla, not at all, but that childish stuff you pack into your brain."

They all got out of the luxurious car. Roxie stood for a moment on that porch, taking everything in.

"Beveled glass edges on the windows," she said appreciatively, "a door that looks like it was taken from some medieval castle. The floor of this porch has been recently redone. No wonder you think God has blessed you."

Carla knew how Roxie meant that last sentence but she had promised herself that she would not allow any more bickering so that everyone's attention would be focussed on Kyle's performance that evening.

Carla's butler opened the door, greeted them and stepped aside as they entered.

"My oh my!" Roxie gasped, forgetting the hard-bitten facade that had been her trademark.

The crystal chandelier set in the circular high ceiling was incontestably the biggest she had ever seen.

"Handmade," Carla told her. "Diamond experts worked on each piece."

"There are *hundreds* of pieces!" Roxie observed. "Are you saying that *each* one was cut like a precious diamond?"

"You got it," Carla agreed.

She asked the butler to pull the drapes and turn on the lights that were set in the chandelier.

A minute later, the visitors were being treated to a sight that left them briefly unable to speak.

A foyer turned into a magical place!

As a result of the meticulous work by the cutters, each hanging crystal, reflecting light, seemed like the most brilliant of flawless diamonds, filling that section of the house with iridescent colors that were lustrous, rainbowlike.

Roxie had to lean against her husband in order to keep from falling because her knees were threatening to give way.

"Oh, Carla..." she finally said.

"I hope you don't think I believe crystals have any mystical properties," Carla laughed. "I designed that chandelier for the sheer beauty of it."

Roxie stood under the exact center of that cavalcade of countless combinations of colors.

"If I could believe that heaven was anything like this," she muttered.

"Roxie..." Carla started to say something but thought better of it, wanting her friend to enjoy that moment unspoiled.

The butler offered to show them to their room on the

third floor, and Roxie and Irving nodded, thanking Carla for her hospitality before they followed behind him.

For a moment the foyer was deserted, no sound except *tick-tick-tick.*

Carla glanced at the antique grandfather's clock in an alcove just below the circular staircase.

It had been in her family for two generations.

And now Kyle and I will be able to pass it on to our children, she thought, nerves tingling all over her body as she considered being the mother of those children. Despite two previous marriages, she had never become pregnant though her very expensive doctors assured her that the fault must have been in her mates.

Forty minutes...

They would have to leave in forty minutes in order to reach the college, and not miss any of Kyle's performance.

Carla opened the front door and walked outside.

Fireflies.

They were out in force that night.

I used to try to trap you in a bottle, she recalled. *I actually succeeded once, and was so happy that I couldn't hardly wait to get back inside to show Momma and Papa. But I tripped, breaking the bottle and killing the little creature inside. It was days before I recovered from that tragedy.*

...we'll have a lifetime ahead of us.

After changing her clothes and reapplying some makeup, Carla stood in the middle of her bedroom, which was more than a thousand square feet. She looked around at her surroundings, the plush Italian provincial furniture, the expensive handwoven draperies, the Venetian marble-endowed bathroom, with its eighteen-karat gold faucets, and combination intercom-and-telephone system. This is the kind of world Kyle will enter when they were married, she realized

since he would not ask her to give up everything and share
his own. But her world was replete with status symbols and
dripping with insincerity, a world that could not have been
more removed from all that he had known for the twenty-
six years of his life, where the traditional value system es-
chewed much of what was taken for granted in her own
life.

This world could swallow you up, she thought of the
young man who was now heading toward the college where
they all would gather in less than two hours. *You might
lose everything that makes you what you are, everything I
love.*

Except his faith.

Carla saw in that faith the greatest possible hope that
Kyle would survive. If anything, he might change some
small part of her world rather than the other way around,
for his personality was so fresh and exciting that he seemed
capable of having great impact upon almost anyone, especially those show business types who thought that they had
seen everyone or everything during their long careers.

But am I being thoroughly honest with you? she asked
herself. *Have I told you all that you should know about the
pressures?*

That was her biggest remaining concern, that she had
unintentionally whitewashed some aspects of the way she
lived and worked. Had she told Kyle about the half-dressed
fans who would throw themselves at him, chipping away
moment by moment at his standard of morality? And then
Carla realized that she had left out none of this.

If Kyle hit big, as she was convinced he would, what
about the pace of one-nighters in state after state, the in-
cessant need to stay up when his energies were down?
Which meant that someone somewhere would offer to Kyle
innocent-looking capsules that would take care of the
"problem."

"My love, my love," Carla spoke out loud, "what kind of Pandora's box am I opening for you?"

And yet it did not end there, this dreary mental list of potential obstacles that she was constructing.

"What if your career zooms, and mine plummets?" she asked. "Can my ego stand that, fragile as it is? Or will it run roughshod over you so often that you will want no part of me after awhile?"

Carla was not kidding herself.

She had been attracted by Kyle's goodness and decency. What would happen if that was worn down, and ultimately did not exist? Would she accept whatever was left? And would he hate her for helping to take it away from him?

And there was the far more immediate worry: would Irving Chicolte actually like Kyle?

Other agents could be approached but by then people undoubtedly would be asking: *Why are you coming to us? Didn't your own agent think this guy was good enough?*

"Do I really *want* you to become a star?" she asked.

But then she was not some sort of Nashville seer. Kyle had introduced her to his faith, and the Lord Who was at the center of it. The answers she did not have must be left in His hands. And perhaps any other questions of the sort that had been assaulting her need not even be asked if she could learn to trust Him enough.

Chapter Six

"They seem normal enough," Roxie observed offhandedly as she walked down the long pathway to Winslow's main arena. "Perhaps better groomed, I must admit, but otherwise not different from kids on other campuses."

"Spoken as though you've got a lot of experience in places like this," Irving Chicolte joked, not sure whether he should be amused by his wife's attitude about the Christian college or irritated by it.

"There is a fascinating *mixture* of students here," Carla told her. "You should realize that not everyone shares a single spiritual viewpoint. This college, one of the older ones, has students enrolled with a wide range of religious backgrounds."

"Well I haven't opened a Bible in years," Irving announced. "Have you?" he asked his wife. "When I wasn't looking perhaps?"

She turned away from him.

"Roxie, *have* you?" he repeated.

"Yes..." she acknowledged reluctantly.

"When?"

"A few days ago."

Now Carla had an idea about what was going on inside her friend's head, and asked, "After we got the prognosis about your condition?"

"Please answer, dear," Irving prodded, never having seen his wife act as she was doing just then.

"Yes, the two of you!" Roxie snapped. "That *is* when I opened a copy of the Bible. Is that something terrible for me to do?"

"But—but you were just arguing with—" he stammered.

Roxie would say nothing further until they were inside the auditorium where Kyle would be singing.

Carla hesitated for a second or two, knowing what she would face as soon as people recognized her. A friend of hers, who was a prominent wrestler-actor, once said, "Carla, how in the world do I go anywhere incognito, will you tell me that? These other guys can slip by and nobody would notice!"

For her part, Carla tried to dress as nondescriptly as possible, wearing a dark tan-colored business-suit-type outfit with plain slacks, instead of the more colorful blouses, dresses and the like toward which she was ordinarily inclined, on and offstage.

Only her long red hair could give her away.

And it did.

Attention was drawn to Carla the moment she entered the auditorium, which held an audience of a thousand, most of the seats already taken. Not everyone got up and congregated around her, asking for autographs, but many did.

I hope they stop before Kyle goes onstage, she thought.

Roxie had the same idea.

"Carla?" she asked.

"Yes, Roxie?"

"It would be a shame if all this attention gave your

friend the idea that people came not so much to hear him but to see you.''

"Roxie!" interjected Irving. "Just because—"

"I'm dying? Is that what you were going to say?"

He looked away, embarrassed.

"That gives me the right to say whatever I please," she asserted. "I wasn't being nasty, Irving. I was trying to warn Carla."

Fortunately those seeking an autograph had gone back to their seats. Carla, Roxie and Irving were still standing in the lobby.

Roxie put her hands on Carla's shoulders.

"You've been around a long time," she said, "but I've got you beat. Ego is a terrible taskmaster. It can be stretched like a hot air balloon or flattened in an instant. If Kyle is the catch of the decade, as you seem to think, it would be a shame to—"

The lights were being turned down.

"Quiet!" Irving insisted. "We'd better get to our seats."

The three of them hurried down to the middle of the auditorium where their seats had been especially reserved.

"I picked these because Kyle will know where we're sitting," Carla told her companions.

"Everything's been planned, I see," Roxie whispered. "You shouldn't expect anything from me, you know. That sounds cruel but it's true, Carla. I'm here out of just a smidgen of curiosity, nothing more."

"I understand, nothing more, that's right, Roxie."

"Remember that when the evening's over."

Roxie returned her attention to the stage, arms folded against her breasts as she awaited Kyle's appearance.

Spotlights were trained on the surprisingly large stage.

Two girls were chattering in their seats behind Carla, Roxie and Irving.

"What a stud!" one of them said.

"Yeah, I know. And to think that he's going to marry an older—"

"*Shush!*" someone nearby said, pointing to Carla in the front seat.

"Geez!" both students said at the same time, slumping down in their seats, both of them blushing nearly as brightly red as Carla's hair.

My darling, she thought. *It doesn't matter what they say or think. You and I are together because it's the Lord's will, in sickness and in health, for richer or—*

Now it was Carla's turn to blush. She felt as though they had already gone through the marriage ceremony.

"Just a few minutes now," an attractive brunette sitting in front of them whispered as the members of the Winslow Orchestra took their places.

Her companion, a younger round-faced woman with close-cropped brown hair, turned and smiled as she said, "I hear he's really remarkable."

"Me, too," the brunette said. "Better than all those other guys with their obnoxious inflated egos."

"That's a tall order to fill. But can they really be compared? Kyle Rivers doesn't sing only country western. He does some gospel, and every so often, he rips into a show tune like 'Memory' or 'Impossible Dream.'"

"That's because he's got the power to do that other stuff."

The orchestra was nearly ready. All talking ceased.

A single spotlight cast a large circle onto the stage, though for a few seconds no one appeared.

Come on, Carla thought. *Don't wait too long.*

A voice. A powerful voice.

While not of operatic type or quality, it was nevertheless strong and so powerful that the volume on the speaker system had to be discreetly turned down.

"How can I say thanks," Kyle's voice rolled over the audience, "for the things You have done for me?"

It was a simple start, beautiful words, building slowly.

"Things so undeserved, Yet You gave to prove Your love for me. The voices of a million angels could not express my gratitude."

Still only the voice, that rich, passionate tenor's voice.

Carla smiled.

Some of the old-line types, the old maids and others will be amazed at just how much power and energy Kyle exudes. If they were expecting some sort of mediocre talent with a pleasant voice, they'll never know what hit them. My Kyle sings with more passion than most of them can imagine.

Suddenly the spotlights merged into one, the beam shrinking until it was only a small patch of light in the darkness of that stage, light trained on a face, then expanding until Kyle's body was fully lit as he sat on a stool, with no musical instrument, only a cordless microphone in his hand.

A number of the members of the audience gasped, then, embarrassed, became silent, unmoving.

Go get 'em, my love, Carla told herself, glad that Kyle had consulted with her about his performance, an area in which she had had more than a decade of experience in every type of venue.

She glanced quickly at Roxie Chicolte whose gaze was trained right at the stage, her mouth partway open. Irving seemed just about equally transfixed.

Impulsively Roxie reached over and grabbed his arm.

Praise God, Carla thought. *Oh, Lord, may her heart be melted!*

"'Great is Thy faithfulness, O God my Father!'" Kyle was singing, his voice building. "'There is no shadow of turning with Thee. Thou changest not, Thy compassion, they fail not...'"

And then the power of Kyle's voice soared, forcing the sound engineers to further cut the volume. A young woman got up from her seat and ran, crying, from the auditorium.

"I wonder what's wrong with her?" asked Irving.

"It's hard to tell," Carla whispered. "He has that effect on some people, impacting them where they live."

They returned their attention to the stage.

"'...Pardon for sin and a peace that endureth,'" Kyle continued. "'Thine own clear presence to cheer and to guide, strength for today in bright passion, they fail not.'"

A few seconds more, and he was finished.

"Chorus!" someone shouted. *"Chorus!"*

Kyle sang the high-volume chorus three more times before the audience, nearly all on their feet, shouting their approval as he finally held up both hands and politely requested that they sit down.

This was the first look most of the men and women in that auditorium had ever had of a largely unknown young singer named Kyle Rivers. They had been conditioned at Winslow to being "entertained" mostly by lacklustre beginners, glorified "Star Search" hopefuls, ninety-eight percent of whom were doomed to anonymity for the rest of their lives.

Kyle did show some resemblance to an actor who had just been named handsomest man in the world by a weekly national magazine, but Kyle was taller by four and a half inches, his face thinner, his eyes more aquamarine than ordinary blue, and he was very broad-shouldered, the formfitting white shirt he wore emphasizing the results of his regular workouts, three days a week in the nearest gym.

I could make love to you right now, Carla thought. *Oh, Lord, help me show some restraint until we are married.*

They had talked about going to Hawaii on their honeymoon, holding one another tightly as the water from a fifty-foot-high waterfall flowed over them; walking hand in hand along an ancient black-sand beach just as the sun set, sending its golden fingers over that isolated spot; and surfing the North Side, or, rather, Carla resting on the hot sand as Kyle showed off the skill he had honed while spending a summer in Orlando, Florida.

"I want to introduce myself," he told the thousand-plus people of all ages present in that auditorium. "I'm Kyle Rivers, from good old Nashville, Tennessee, home to the best music in America."

Smiling broadly, he added, "Sorry, Metropolitan Opera."

The audience lost any reserve it had left, acting almost as a single entity while giving Kyle a standing ovation.

Finally, they all sat down again.

"And now my very next number will be 'Achy Breaky Heart,'" he said, obviously kidding.

Collective booing arose from the audience.

"Actually, I'll do another," Kyle told them, chuckling. "'You Light Up My Life.' I'm going to sing it not as though it was intended for some woman this time, but to God Himself. For, you see, He *does* light up my life."

The audience was quiet this time, absorbing every word he sang, every note played by the orchestra.

As Kyle finished, women were taking handkerchiefs out of their purses and wiping their eyes.

Including Roxie Chicolte.

"The air's not very pure in here," she said defensively.

"Why do you say that?" her husband asked.

"Dust or something...I got a speck in my eye."

"Roxie, Roxie, you and a hundred others!"

She avoided her husband's knowing gaze and tried instead to concentrate on the stage eleven aisles in front of where she was sitting, as much attention as she could muster focused on Kyle Rivers, whose appearance utterly disarmed her, surprised as she was by his overwhelming handsomeness.

Though Roxie was easily old enough to be his grandmother, she found him mesmerizing. Helping Irving with his business, she'd met so many actors who usually were not half as interesting as this gifted man sitting on a simple stool, with no other props around him.

Irving was sitting next to Carla, and Roxie impulsively leaned over him to whisper to her, "I can see why you find this guy exciting. Any woman would have to be brain-dead not to agree!"

"Thank you!" Carla exclaimed. "What you see is *less* than what you get. There is so much more to Kyle."

Carla settled back in her chair, especially pleased that Roxie apparently was not going to stay upset with her.

Lord, she prayed silently, *a cold heart isn't an easy one to get through to. I need Your help.*

Until Kyle began his next number, she let her mind roam a bit.

The way he was dressed on stage had changed from the first time she'd seen him. Now he seemed to be emphasizing his looks more than he had done previously, which must have been why he decided to wear a stark white shirt, that showed off the width of his shoulders and chest, to be sure. His jeans were black, and he wore smooth black leather boots.

You are becoming more aware of your effect on audiences, she told herself, *which in the short run is good but it could lead to real arrogance and, eventually, a plastic personality like so many others before you. Please, please, be careful, my love. Don't sacrifice what is real about you.*

Kyle continued singing with numbers that ranged from "Like the Rain" and "I Can Still Make Cheyenne," to "Little Bitty." But he did not stop with those. He went

beyond country and gospel to do Broadway numbers that
included two songs from *Evita*.

"I can't believe it!" an older woman sitting to Carla's
right exclaimed. "I just can't. How can he do it? From
country to show tunes to gospel, he's fantastic!"

The gray-haired, bearded man next to her whispered,
"This kid seems inspired, hon. Angels couldn't do better."

A smile crossed Carla's face, then, abruptly, she felt a
hand rest gently on her shoulder, startling her.

Turning her head a bit, she asked, "Can I help you?"

"Just enjoying the show," replied the student behind
her.

"You didn't tap me on the shoulder?" she persisted,
quite sure that someone *had* touched her.

"No, ma'am."

"Sorry."

"Not a problem. Your boyfriend is great!"

"Thank you very much."

Embarrassed, Carla slumped down in her seat. Irving
leaned over and asked, "What was that all about?"

"Nothing," she said.

"Are you sure?" Irving pressed, knowing after so many
years in show business when *anyone* was being evasive.

"I am."

Kyle had three other songs to deliver but for the first
time during one of his performances, Carla found that her
attention was straying from the golden boy on stage to
something else entirely.

The hand on her shoulder.

She had no doubt that someone *had* touched her.

Yet why would no one admit it? she asked herself. *Are
they nervous about having bothered a celebrity?*

Carla assumed that that was the problem, and tried to get
the incident out of her mind. But it would not leave her

alone. She decided to ask Kyle when the two of them were alone, and no one could overhear.

I wonder if— she thought, then felt something cold race along her spine until it disappeared just as quickly.

Strangely enough, despite her newness in the faith that they now shared, Carla suspected what Kyle might tell her but it was an answer she did not want to confront until it could no longer be avoided.

Chapter Seven

Chapter Seven

Kyle Rivers intended to end his performance at Winslow Christian College that evening with a rendition of "Amazing Grace."

He paused before starting, and it seemed as though his strong but tired body was newly invigorated, something more than mere adrenaline surging through him.

"'Amazing grace!'" Kyle sang, his face lighting up with a magical smile. "'How sweet the sound that saved a wretch like me!'"

Almost inexplicably, he started weeping but not theatrical tears, appearing on cue to add drama to that moment.

"Hold on!" he said, waving at the orchestra to stop playing.

Carla sat up straight in her seat.

Whatever Kyle was doing then had not been in any way planned between the two of them.

There's got to be a structure to any good act, her mind shouted at him. *Everything in place. You shouldn't be doing this, you shouldn't—*

"The Lord wants me to tell you something," Kyle said,

his voice clear and strong over the massive loudspeakers ringing that auditorium. "He wants me to say that I have come to Winslow tonight with the wrong spirit."

He gazed out over the mass of forms barely visible in the unbroken darkness beyond the stage.

"I came here to show you what *I* could do," he told them, "to impress you with *my* talent."

As he hesitated, trying to make sense out of the jumble of emotions he was beginning to feel, someone shouted back at him, "What's wrong with that? God gave you your talent, didn't he?"

Kyle was caught by surprise but seemed to know the answer instinctively.

"Yes, my brother, he did," he managed to reply. "Without Him in my life and His gifts, I would be nothing."

"Then how can that be the wrong spirit, I mean, you doing what your talent enables you to do so wonderfully?" the same male student asked, genuinely wanting to know, to learn. "How many other entertainers radiate the joy of faith that you have been doing throughout this evening?"

"But, my brother, my talent, yes, given to me by God is supposed to be for *His* honor and glory, not something to build *me* up. If I am the focus, then I am the problem."

The student who had been speaking stepped out into the aisle.

"You are the most humble performer I have ever seen or heard," the young man said as he walked forward a few feet, his own cheeks wet with tears. "Even when you sing tunes that are not overtly spiritual, you do so in a way that draws our attention somehow to the One Who planted that voice within you."

"But everyone here is thinking about me," Kyle told him.

"Maybe so. But we are the *vessels*. The message is carried *through* us. We cannot cut ourselves out of the picture.

If some of the acclaim splashes over on us, that can't be avoided. What is important is how we feel inside.

"You may have come to Winslow with the wrong spirit but that spirit has fled, Kyle Rivers, it is no longer there. Be thankful for that, be very thankful, man. It is God's grace that comes through you now, so loud and clear that angels must be rejoicing in heaven because of what is happening."

Kyle had stepped down from the stage, and was walking toward the young man.

"What is your name?" he asked.

"Darien."

Kyle reached out and hugged him.

"My brother Darien is right!" he acknowledged.

He hugged the other young man a final time, then headed back to the stage.

Nearly all of those in the audience were on their feet again, singing, "'I once was lost but now am found, was blind but now I see.'"

Carla had joined in and was singing along with them. Then, oddly, everyone else in the audience stopped, leaving only Kyle and she to tackle the remaining stanzas of "Amazing Grace," he on stage, she from where she had been sitting.

Kyle was handed another mike by someone in the wings, which he threw to Carla with such accuracy that she caught it in one hand.

And sing together the two of them did, yet that moment had not been rehearsed! They seemed so in sync with one another it was easy to imagine they had been together all their lives, not just a few weeks. They had not even rehearsed "Amazing Grace" but they sang it with such soaring passion that, after they had finished, no one in the auditorium could move or say anything to one another but were emotionally depleted from listening.

Kyle motioned for Carla to join him on stage.

As soon as she wrapped her arm around his waist, and he rested his on her shoulders, the audience started clapping, and shouting, "More! More! More!"

"We're so tired," Kyle called out to them. "Another time, please."

But a thousand people would not relent. The ovation continued unabated.

He pulled away from Carla and held his arms out in front of him.

"All right, all right," he said, "if I sing a really special, brand-new song right now, will you let us go?"

The audience reaction was unmistakable, a near deafening shout of "Yes, Kyle!"

"Carla," he said, "I've written a song to present to you tonight. I want you to sit down while I sing it to you."

He pointed to an extra chair in the orchestra pit. Someone handed it up to him.

"Please sit down, Carla," he told her. "I want everyone here to know how I *really* feel about you."

None of what Kyle was doing had been rehearsed.

He got down on his knees in front of her.

"I don't worship you, my love," he said, "for that would be very wrong but I do adore you so much. I think about you when I wake up in the morning, and when I go to sleep at night. And sometimes I dream about you. I've written a song. It's dedicated to you. I want to sing it now, for the first time in public."

He took her small, rather fragile-looking hand in his own and kissed the back of it.

"I'm calling this, 'Love Is a River,'" he announced. "I wrote it last night and went to sleep singing it."

And as soon as Kyle began, all the other songs he had performed that evening were eclipsed by this one number, with the exception of "My Tribute: To God be the Glory" and "Amazing Grace," words of profound devotion pouring from him as though they were utterly unstoppable. At first he did so without music, then the orchestra quickly picked up on the melody and was able to accompany him.

For five minutes, he expressed his love for Carla through the power of song, and if it had been possible, no one in the Winslow College auditorium would have taken time even to breathe for they were entranced by the sheer ardor of what he was doing, singing with mind, body and soul to this flame-haired woman, singing of all the joy he felt when the two of them were together.

Just once Kyle broke away from words sung to words simply spoken.

"I know we will not live perfectly," he said. "I know we will not love God and one another completely. There is only One Who can be perfect, and only once, in Eden, when human beings had a one-time chance at perfection. But I also know that I will never stop loving you, whatever your imperfections, my beloved, and I pray, God knows how *much* I pray, that you will somehow get past my own shortcomings and not lose patience."

Carla stood up and kissed him right there on stage as passionately as she had ever kissed him before.

"My love, my life..." Her words were picked up by the microphone.

And then Kyle continued on with the rest of "Love Is a River."

After he was finished, he stood, Carla beside him, the two of them holding hands, as the people in the auditorium responded with a sustained round of applause that lasted nearly as long as the song itself.

"God bless you all!" Kyle said, throwing everybody a kiss.

Just as they were turning to go backstage, someone

shouted, "The Lord has blessed me already by letting me be here tonight, praise God!"

Another said something very much like that, but with even stronger emotion. And a third followed. More and more people stood and shouted whatever was in their hearts, not caring what anybody else thought.

Kyle held up both hands, and shouted, "I want to say something else."

After they quieted down, he told them, "To God be the glory, remember that always, not Kyle Rivers, not Carla Gearhart, no one but the Father of us all!"

One pair of hands clapping was joined by another, and the applause started all over again.

"Peace and joy to you all," Kyle added before Carla and he left the stage and made it to his dressing room.

They joyously collapsed into one another's arms.

Later, until past midnight, as well as during the days to follow, houses and cafés and dorms and offices and churches and homes were filled with conversation about the phenomenon at Winslow Christian College that evening, for none had ever before experienced anything like it.

On the way home, Roxie and Irving Chicolte were quieter than usual.

Mostly the two of them commented about the quality of Kyle's voice and his personal magnetism, but even then they spoke rather tersely. However, Carla knew that there was more going on with them than that. Normally, as well as she knew them both, she could guess that they would be chattering away either praising a particular entertainer or condemning that individual with the cruelest comments. Neither was hesitant about destroying someone's ego and, sometimes, along with that, any hope that person had of a career. Irving was the one in charge of the Hollywood Chicolte Agency but Roxie was never less than exceptionally influential. She had far more impact upon Irving's decisions than did the wives of the top bosses throughout the entertainment business's power elite. Which meant that she was one of the most powerful women in Hollywood since Irving remained one of the two top mover-and-shaker agents.

Once back at the house, they thanked Carla for showing them such a fine evening and then went to their guest quarters.

She watched them disappear up the staircase.

They thought he was terrific, she told herself. What more do I want? They could have hated him, after all.

But after more than a decade's relationship with the Chicoltes, she knew them better than they might have guessed and could tell that everything she saw was on the surface, and something else underneath was far more substantial.

Carla hurried to a phone in her study and dialed Kyle's number.

No answer.

The clock on her desk read 12:05.

"I wonder if anything's happened," she said out loud, a not uncustomary surge of paranoia gripping her. "He must be bone tired. Maybe, when he was driving to his place, he got careless and—"

Carla ordered herself to stop that kind of musing, for in addition to needless worry, it smacked of one of her less desirable qualities—the urge to smother any new relationship, to possess it and eventually suck the life from it. Her past was littered with the spent husks of friendships that she had destroyed by this very tendency.

Think of what you just experienced, she told herself, the impact Kyle had on his audience. Think of that and let the joy of it turn your mind, your heart away from—

What an extraordinary evening! And its aftermath surely

provided the conditions for Kyle not getting back as soon
as he might have otherwise.

Dozens of people, if not more, must have wanted piece
after piece of his time after the performance, strangers who
became instant fans—how could they avoid this after seeing what he could do?—out-of-town reviewers for metropolitan newspapers, perhaps a radio or television inter-
viewer or two.

Calm down, lady, she scolded herself. *He's going to be
your husband, not your lap dog. Give him some space.*

She got ready for bed, then sat on the edge of the mattress, her insides tense.

"I want to hold you all the time," she said as she looked
at an eight-by-ten color shot of Kyle lifting weights, his
body glistening with perspiration. It was in an expensive
mother-of-pearl frame which she had placed on the bureau
dresser opposite her bed, and showed one side of him, rug-
ged, athletic, the hunk side that set her nerve ends tingling.

Another was revealed in the photograph on the night
table next to her. Kyle was standing before a window, sunlight touching his hair and left cheek, and traveling down
his chest and hips. He wore a full-sleeved white shirt, with
the first few buttons open. His expression was one of longing. He wanted her with all his heart—and she felt the same
about him. But they had established a pact between themselves that they would not make love until the first night
of their honeymoon.

It seemed odd at first to Carla. She had never held herself
back from getting involved with men whom she found attractive.

Not this time, for him, for her.

She knew that in agreeing to hold off until they were
married, she was surrendering herself to *his* value system.
In the past, that would never have happened. She had become far too liberated over the years, particularly since she

was earning more money than virtually all the men around her, unless she happened to be sharing the stage with one of the hotshot guys who dominated the country music scene.

Somehow, though, none of this mattered. Somehow, she did not feel as though she were *forcing* herself to do anything. Somehow, she genuinely *wanted* to wait, to keep their relationship pure until they were in their hotel suite in the shadow of Diamond Head, after a wedding ceremony that was bound to be a media event.

No one else knew that this was the case. When the tabloids started publishing photos of the two of them, the headlines for blatantly fictitious articles emphasized the love nest they were maintaining on the outskirts of Nashville, and the torrid weekends they supposedly spent together.

"They don't care about love," Kyle remarked as the flood of tabloid coverage commenced. "They just want to know when and what you and I do in bed. I never realized how sick these rags were until now."

"Because you'd never been the object of any of it," Carla told him, "the tidal wave of filth that threatens any celebrity these days."

"You think I'm all that good-looking?" he asked, not fishing for ego reasons but genuinely unimpressed with his own appearance.

Carla recalled the conversation. They were sitting in the indoor spa at Carla's house. She liked the temperature as hot as possible, and as she looked at him after he asked that question, she knew that the water wasn't the only thing hot then, Kyle's sensuality blatant and nearly overpowering.

"You have no idea, do you, of the effect you have on women?" she asked, dumfounded.

He ignored answering her, as always awkward about discussing such matters.

My naive hunk! she exclaimed to herself. *Does it get any better than this?*

"You don't seem surprised about any of this," Kyle said instead.

"I'm not," she replied. "It's been a part of my life for ten years now. And you had better get used to it."

"Won't it stop or at least be toned down once we're married?" he asked. "The tabloids have all the spicy stuff flying furiously now. But as newlyweds?"

Her expression said it all.

"It will be, if anything, worse, won't it, Carla?"

"You might not think that it *could* be worse but, you're right, what we see in those publications now is nothing compared to what will be happening later. They will dream up extramarital affairs for one or the other or both of us. That you can count on!"

"Then we'll sue them, right?"

"Wrong, Kyle. That only makes them mad. Right now it's just business, a twisted game of sorts with these people. But if we sued, it would turn into something even darker, meaner."

"Revenge, Carla?"

"You hit a bull's-eye, my love."

None of what they were talking about had occurred to Kyle previously. He hesitated for a moment, and she worried that her candor was having exactly the effect that she prayed it would not.

"When we get married, we will promise to love one another for better or for worse," he said finally. "This just belongs to that 'for worse' part. We can't ignore it, Carla. We have to decide whether we'll *really* mean what we will pledge at the ceremony."

As he spoke, Carla felt her heart ache with love for him. She wanted their wedding to be past so that they could begin the honeymoon with all the passion that both had somehow kept under restraint for the weeks they had known each other.

"You are perfect," she said, "you are a perfect man."

"Oh, no, dear Carla, I am not. You just haven't seen all my imperfections."

"I can't imagine anything less than perfect about you," she said honestly.

The phone rang, and the sound of it startled her out of her reverie.

She grabbed for the receiver.

"Hello..." she answered nervously.

"Kyle here," he said. "You sound as though you were expecting the local funeral director to call."

"Don't kid like that, ever!" she yelled and hung up on him, furious, her whole body shivering.

Five seconds later, the phone rang again.

"Sorry..." she said as soon as she could answer it.

"I was going to say the same thing," hê remarked. "Forgive me. I *am* sorry. That was bad, bad humor."

"It was, but I still love you," Carla assured him. "Kyle, how could I ever *stop* loving you?"

He sucked in his breath.

"Remember something for me?" he asked, his voice sounding husky.

"What?"

He was teasing her a bit but there was little that Kyle could do that would really turn her off.

"As you are falling asleep, promise?"

"All right, all right, what's this that you want me to think about tonight?"

"I can't wait to marry you and watch you fall asleep in my arms."

Carla's cheeks grew warm and she could hardly believe it. It had been years since she'd felt herself blush.

Chapter Eight

I need Thy presence every passing hour..."

Carla had been listening to a song over a gospel music station when Irving knocked on the half-open kitchen door.

"Good morning," he said. "No servants to wait on you, breakfast in bed, that sort of thing?"

"Not everyone sees me as you do now," she replied self-consciously, "without a drop of makeup. It's image, you know. They would leave this house and talk, talk, talk. I can't control what they say but I *can* do something about how they see me. That's why they never come here before ten o'clock at the earliest."

"Vanity, Carla," he chided her. "Is that at all consistent with this new outlook of yours on life?"

"I've not thought about it, Irving. I'm just worried about image, I suppose."

"Image? Yes, I know, Carla. I helped to create your image, remember?"

He sat down at the breakfast table with her, and poured some coffee for himself as he turned serious and asked, "Carla, my dear?"

"None of it."

"You knew what I was going to ask."

"As I know you, Irving."

Carla could almost read the man's thoughts by the un-masked expressions playing across his face, none of which he ever tried to suppress, for this was someone who believed that he was the way he was, and that pretense was all too common in his industry, hence he tried like crazy to avoid it.

"None of it was planned, I mean, that special stuff?" he probed, wanting to believe her but not quite convinced.

"Stuff, Irving? Is that all it seemed to you?"

She let her distaste for what he said surface more than she intended but it just seemed a shoddy comment to make.

"Sorry," Irving replied, uncharacteristically contrite.

"Forgiven," she told him.

"Seriously?"

"For sure, Irving."

"You use that word *forgiven* so easily."

"There's no mystery to it," Carla assured him. "I forgive you, my dear. What's the problem?"

"I heard it more than once last night."

"Was it offensive?"

"Sometimes, Carla."

"Why?"

"There is much that can never be forgiven. *Everything* in life isn't subject to it, you know."

"You're wrong, Irving."

"Are you so sure?"

"Absolutely!"

"After just a few weeks, Carla? Be realistic, please. How can you understand the implications in so short a period of time?"

"Kyle says—"

Irving was a little exasperated by Carla's acceptance of whatever Kyle said as automatically true.

"Is this guy always right?" he asked. "I thought you all felt that Jesus was the only perfect Man."

"All right, you have me there," Carla responded, knowing that Irving had chalked up one on his side.

"Then why bring him into this now? Isn't that an easy way to avoid arriving at your own conclusions?" Irving argued not unreasonably.

She was wary of verbally sparring with the man since he had mastered the practice before she was born. All she could do was speak from the center of her soul, and she suspected that he would not be prepared for that, given the superficiality that governed so many relationships in Hollywood.

"In matters of the spirit," Carla told him, "and of the Bible, I think Kyle comes close as close as any man could."

Irving grunted as he replied, "All well and good, dear, and I know you and probably your boyfriend are sincere, but then Kyle is just twenty-six years old, Carla. Frankly I've bumped into a number of clergymen who were three times his age. Aren't you willing to acknowledge that they could have picked up something new during half a century of additional living and learning, and might have insights that have not yet occurred to someone as young as Kyle Rivers?"

Irving's mood was proving considerably more combative than usual, and this for a man for whom verbal fencing was one of life's greater joys.

"You seem testy this morning," Carla snapped. "I mean, you usually are but this is a bit much even so. Was it last night?"

He blinked a couple of times in rapid succession.

"That's it, Irving, I know it is!" she exclaimed. "Admit it, okay?"

He nodded but that was all he was willing to concede.

Carla's tone softened as she asked him, "I thought you enjoyed the performance last night?"

"I did...."

Irving was not looking at her directly, untypically avoiding her eyes while running a finger around the rim of the coffee cup.

"Then what is wrong?" Carla pressed, lowering her voice.

"A cross-examination?" he asked, trying to resurrect his old testy self but not very convincingly.

"I'm just concerned," she told him.

Irving said, "Of course you are. I know that, Carla. Have patience with me this morning, please."

"Always, friend."

"How many of my clients call me that? How many think of me as just a funnel for contracts?"

"No rush, Irving, no pressure," Carla assured him. "I know that you'll tell me when you're ready."

"Well, I'm ready."

She waited, anxious to help him for a change when, usually, their relationship meant that the reverse was true.

"Roxie," he told her, "it's Roxie. She's becoming more and more bitter. In some respects, Kyle intimidates her."

"He had that effect on me at first, you know."

"Really?"

"You bet he did!"

"Maybe she'll change. Right now Roxie worries that Kyle will turn you into some narrow-minded—"

She interrupted him.

"Never that, Irving, and you can take that to the bank," Carla declared.

* * *

Carla had just finished dialing Kyle's apartment number as well as his pager for the twelfth time.

"He must have been held up in traffic," Roxie spoke reassuringly, having come downstairs at last.

"Not at this hour," Carla snapped nervously. She heard something outside, and dashed to the front door, swinging it open.

It was a bright yellow muscle car with glass-packed mufflers racing down the highway adjacent to her property.

"Not Kyle, not Kyle, not Kyle!" she muttered as she slammed the door shut.

Eleven-twenty.

The time indicated on the antique mahogany grandfather clock in the foyer was unmistakable.

Carla glanced from Irving to Roxie.

"I'm overreacting, aren't I?" she asked sheepishly.

"Oh, just a tad!" Roxie agreed, laughing. Carla joined her, and even Irving cracked a smile.

"I'm seeing angels, and you're having a breakdown. Great way to start the day!"

"Angels?" her husband repeated.

Both women abruptly realized that Irving had no idea what it was that his wife was talking about.

"Please, sit down, my dear," Roxie told him. "There really is something you should know."

They retreated to the dining room where Carla's cook would be starting to serve breakfast.

"Now what's this about angels?" Irving asked.

Roxie described the encounter, expecting the man she lived with for nearly four decades to start cackling hysterically, saying something on the order of, "You don't believe in God, yet you've seen an angel. How wild, *how wild!*"

But his response was nothing like that. Instead Irving Chicolte seemed only to be looking into space, as though he had lost contact with everyone and everything around him.

"Darling, are you okay?" Roxie asked.

He nodded but still did not speak immediately.

The phone in the hallway rang. Carla jumped to her feet but her maid, a black woman named Fannie Chisolm, short, heavyset, looking like Hattie McDaniel in *Gone With the Wind*, rushed into the dining room, and almost collided with Carla.

"It's Memorial Hospital!" she exclaimed. "Mr. Kyle's been in an accident. Oh, Miss Carla, he's not expected to live!"

A transformation took hold of Roxie Chicolte.

In an instant she became a substitute, hovering mother for Carla, holding her with great gentleness as the younger woman sobbed hysterically on the way to Nashville Memorial Hospital which was thirty miles from where she lived.

"The price of isolation from my public," Carla mumbled. "If I were an ordinary person we'd have been there before now."

Roxie held her while Carla's chauffeur drove the Bentley as fast as he could manage, using a couple of shortcuts.

...he's not expected to live!

The words cut through Carla's newfound faith like a chainsaw, ripping it to pieces.

"How could God allow this to happen to us?" she cried out.

Roxie could say little. She did not have the foundation to help Carla on a spiritual level. But she did what she could.

"I lost my brother twenty years ago," she spoke softly. "Other than Irving, he was the man I had loved the most in my life. I didn't know how I could ever survive without him. For forty years, Manny was there with me.

"After Irving swept me off my feet, and we were finally

married, Manny and I talked three or four times a day by phone, often more than that. We saw each other maybe half a dozen times a week. He was as natural a part of my world as eating or breathing. And, then, suddenly, he was gone.''

Roxie tensed as some of the old memories, especially precious ones, surfaced for the first time in years. She had buried them in the hope that she could reduce the pain that she carried with her but, invariably, in emotional moments, even as she would go off by herself to calm down, her mind would roam, and she would see him, smiling, with such vividness that it was not difficult for her to imagine that he had actually returned somehow, and that she could reach and he'd be there in the flesh.

''I wasn't such a cold dame before my brother Manny's death,'' she said, hoping to shift Carla's attention momentarily away from Kyle. ''But one of the two best men in my life was wiped out because of some slobbering drunk driving too fast, ignoring a stop sign and hitting poor Manny's car on the driver's side—just about tearing in two.

''I decided that loving anyone other than Irving represented too much of a risk. I knew the answer to that question, 'Is it better to have loved and lost than never to have loved at all?' hands on, no debate. My husband gave me all the warm, loving companionship that I needed. My heart would be labeled No Trespassing from then on.''

Roxie sighed resignedly.

''That's the way it's been for twenty long years now,'' she acknowledged. ''Nobody gets any more of a piece of me than I am willing to give. That's why whatever friends I have these days could admit to the last one of them, 'Roxie's nice and all, but we feel as though we don't really know her. She walls off a large part of who she really is, and nobody can get *really* close to her.'''

Carla had been silent while listening to her friend.

"But I'm different," she spoke up finally. "I *need* people. I'm somebody who's *always* needed them."

"But what has that gotten you now?" Roxie queried. "Is it worth *this*? I mean, look at what you're going through. We get a short while of joy followed by what seems a lifetime of anguish. I don't like the odds."

"But what alternative could there be?" Carla argued. "I mean, Roxie, look at what you've—"

"Become? Is that what you were going to say?"

Carla's defenses and good judgment were messed up since part of her was reaching out to Kyle and desperately hoping that the doctors were wrong, and that he would pull through after all.

"I'm sorry," she apologized. "Forgive me, please."

"For telling the truth? Why should you be forgiven that? You're right. I'm a shriveled up hag, Carla. I get by because I'm meaner than anybody around me. I can make the worst showbiz egomaniac back down in a New York minute.

"Tough old Irving here is a sweetheart compared to the likes of me. When he needs help, he sends in the company witch—me, of course. You see, I do have a purpose in life! Not everybody does!"

Carla's attention shifted briefly from Kyle and focussed on this woman who was holding her with such tenderness, and yet talking as though Medusa would cower in fear before a glance from her.

If Kyle is dead by the time we reach his room, she thought, *will I allow myself to become what she is? Is that what I want as his legacy?*

She had been leaning against Roxie's shoulder but straightened up as the other woman handed her a pink lace-fringed handkerchief.

"That's pretty," Carla told her after using it to wipe her eyes.

"My grandmother gave it to me. I carry it everywhere I go. She died on my twelfth birthday."

"How old was she?"

"Nearly a hundred."

"A hundred years old?"

"And pretty healthy until the end. But I guess that sweet lady's heart was weaker than anybody knew."

Roxie's love for her grandmother broke through layers of crassness that were integral to her frigid personality.

"Both sets of my grandparents are still alive," Carla mused. "I've never had to face letting go."

"You are very fortunate to have avoided—" Roxie started to say.

"Pardon me, but it's just another mile or so before we reach the hospital," the chauffeur interrupted reluctantly.

Carla thanked him, then tapped Irving on the shoulder.

"You don't have to hang around, waiting for me," she told him. "Rocco can take you back home."

"And waste this trip?" Irving told her. "It'll never happen, my dear."

Less than a minute passed before her British-made luxury car pulled up in front of the hospital. Carla did not wait for the door to be opened for her.

No reporters, which was something of a miracle in itself.

But her doctor, Thornton Fowler, a man well over six feet tall, with the build of a basketball player, was waiting for her at the entrance.

"Is Kyle—?" she started to say.

"He's holding on, Miss Gearhart."

She had hired him to take care of her parents and, in fact, her entire household and office staff.

"Is that an honest report," she demanded, "or one of your well-rehearsed medical euphemisms?"

Dr. Fowler regretted that she knew him as well as she did.

"Sorry…" he told her. "Yes, Kyle Rivers *is* holding on but not for much longer, I'm afraid."

"How much time does he have?"

He winced as he gave her an honest answer but a harsh one.

"A few hours," the doctor spoke.

Carla stifled a gasp.

"Or less?" she pressed.

"Probably less," the doctor acknowledged.

"Is he conscious?"

"At times."

She started to walk past him.

"Miss Gearhart," Dr. Fowler said as he touched her shoulder. "There is something else."

She faced him again, her eyes bloodshot, mascara and other makeup trickling down her cheeks.

He hesitated, then told her, "It can wait."

"No, it *can't* wait," she said. "I don't want to face this and then, if he recovers, have you hit me with something else. I want it all now!"

"When we started treating him, we found that he is at the early stages of a condition involving a degenerative nerve syndrome."

"In plain English, please!"

"Even if Kyle lives, he will eventually lose all control of his body."

Carla could feel the floor slipping out from under her.

"Are you saying paralysis?" she asked.

The doctor shook his head.

"Not that," he said simply.

"Then what is it?"

"Something that might be considered worse."

"Worse than—?"

"Yes…"

"Go ahead. Just tell me."

She knew the doctor was trying to be protective, recognizing that she was more vulnerable than usual. "Look, I know where you're coming from. But this is harder on me than letting me have the whole ball of wax right away."

"It's a distant cousin to leprosy but without the twisted and missing limbs, without the boils and such. The link is that leprosy is not all of those things that people have supposed over the years but, rather, deadening of the body's nerves."

He hesitated, feeling the strain of what he had to tell her, and not being able to go on for a moment or two.

Carla's own nerve endings seemed to be frozen, and she was finding it hard to breathe, numbness covering most of her body.

"What about his body now?" she asked finally.

"It's fine. There is just no telling when the condition will worsen."

"And what will happen to him when it does?"

"He will just collapse, Carla, and he will be unable to control his body."

Abruptly that hospital corridor seemed to start spinning around in her vision, and she fell against Dr. Fowler.

"Oh, dear—what's happening to me?" she asked, prepared for the worst possible answer that he could give.

"Stress, I suspect, Miss Gearhart, nothing more. You should rest a bit before going in to see him."

The doctor had put his arms around her to steady her but now she was pulling away from him.

"I won't wait another minute!" she declared.

"Then at least let me walk with you, in case you have another episode. Take my arm," he told her.

Since she still felt wobbly, she took the doctor's arm and allowed him to help her down the hall.

Carla had to admit to herself that she could not have made it to the elevator without Dr. Fowler's strength to hold her up. And she saw him give a stern expression to any staff members who seemed unusually curious.

As the four of them stepped into the elevator, Carla Gearhart, the most successful female country music singer in history and the only one to have won an Oscar for Best Actress, felt for a moment some sudden and irrational sensation that she had entered a tomb and it was closing around her.

Chapter Nine

Carla wasn't sure that she wanted to go into Kyle's hospital room after all.

During the few weeks she knew him, he had seemed to be completely self-sufficient, so tall and handsome, with a physique that would have put any motion picture heartthrob to shame. She felt reassured simply by being next to him, by the firmness and strength of his body as he held her. She never thought she could be swept away by any man ever again, but Kyle Rivers had done that, a man brimming over with masculinity yet vulnerable enough that the child in him was never far from the surface.

And yet, despite the chemistry between them, despite their strong passion, they had not made love, and would not until they were married.

But now Kyle was being taken from her without the chance of any union between them.

How could she go into his room and see him there, connected to a myriad of tubes and whatever else, see him like a baby in a kind of institutional womb, just as helpless, just as unaware of what was going on around him? At least, *with a baby, there was the beauty of life beginning, not the tragedy of its end....*

Roxie, Irving and Dr. Fowler stayed outside while Carla quietly entered Kyle's room only to find him in the midst of a crisis as two nurses tried to revive him.

Hearing the confusion, Dr. Fowler rushed in, and took charge.

"His heart has stopped!" he yelled. "Get me—"

Carla backed up against the wall, her own heart pounding.

"Oh, God, God!" she cried out with real pain. "It wasn't supposed to be like this. We thought You—"

Dr. Fowler applied pressure to Kyle's chest by hand since the right machine happened to be at the other end of the hospital.

"Injection now!' he ordered, "in the area of the heart. Hurry! I can't do this again because of his condition."

The needle was the longest one Carla had ever seen.

"What are you doing?" she begged.

"Trying to get his heart started again by shocking it into a reaction to the drug my nurse is administering."

Seconds passed.

"Flat-lining," one of the nurses whispered to Dr. Fowler, and he nodded after looking at the same machine beside his bed.

The doctor was about to turn and face Carla when the second nurse tugged on his sleeve, adding, "Wait, Doctor! Look at the screen!" as she pointed frantically to the TV-like instrument resting on a special heavy-duty metal stand next to Kyle's bed.

The unmoving green line in the center jumped once, twice, a third time.

"Praise God!" Carla exclaimed. "Praise His holy name. Thank you, Lord, oh, thank you, Jesus."

The two nurses and the doctor exchanged stunned glances.

"No, it's flat-lining again!" Dr. Fowler observed a few seconds afterwards. "That was only reflexive movement...means nothing."

Out of desperation, feeling as though she were at the point of death herself, Carla stood up straight. She hurried across the room to Kyle's bedside but she felt as though she were walking through sand, each step requiring strength that was quickly flowing out of her, until she heard what Dr. Fowler felt he was forced to declare.

"Kyle's gone!" he told her. "Carla, he's—"

For a moment, Carla's gaze and his seemed to lock, in part because this was the first time in the ten years they had known each other that he had called her "Carla". He hoped that he could keep her from a breakdown episode on the spot. As far as he was concerned, Kyle Rivers *was* gone, another lost patient, however harsh and sad that fact was to confront.

The nurses grabbed Carla and tried very hard to restrain her but she would have none of this.

"Miss Gearhart, he's dead!" one of them yelled. "You've got accept that and calm down."

"*No!*" Carla said. "Let me go. I must hold his hand. I must tell him how much I love him. I must pray that—"

The nurses tried to hold Carla back, but she broke free, and reached the bed. She grabbed Kyle's left hand as she closed her eyes.

"Lord, please, don't take him!" she sobbed. "He's everything I need in my life apart from You."

The nurses and Dr. Fowler seemed frozen where they stood.

Nothing had changed. Kyle was still not breathing, the screen next to the bed showing the same response as before: a flat line where there should have been fluctuation.

"Carla, give it up!" Dr. Fowler pleaded. "We've lost him. You could do yourself harm by not accepting that fact. Please, think of the other people who—"

She spun around and faced him.

"If I give him up now, my own life might as well be over, and I will be no good to anyone," she said. "If I have to stand before his coffin and kiss his cold forehead before the lid is closed, and I never see him again in *this* world, you should bury me right next to him because that *will* be the end."

"Would Kyle have wanted that?" he asked. "Would he have wished *anything* like that for you?"

"Of course he wouldn't, we both know that," she told him. "I just feel, God knows how deeply, that his life and mine are now woven together, and I can't help feeling the way I do, I just can't—"

A hand. On her shoulder. Just as she had felt in the arena earlier.

Carla spun around, thinking that it was Kyle's hand but his form remained rigid, his eyes closed.

A voice again.

Fear not....

Seconds passed. Then—

Carla felt that she was in that hospital room and yet not in it, felt that she was a bystander witnessing the drama as well as a participant in it, felt that she was being torn between the finite and the infinity.

"Look!" one of the two nurses shouted. "Look at the scope!"

The flat line was jumping, peaking, then falling back, peaking again, then—

"What's happening?" the other nurse spoke.

Dr. Fowler rushed over to them. "His heart's beating again!" he exclaimed. "But, look, it's almost as though he's

having some sort of struggle.'' He sucked in his breath,
flabbergasted at what he was seeing.

"I've never witnessed anything like this,'' he said,
stunned.

"What do we do?'' both the nurses inquired at once.

"I'm at a loss, I—''

More seconds.

None of those in the room noticed at first but a crowd
had been gathering in the corridor outside, including more
than one of the interns, doctors and nurses sticking their
heads past the doorway.

The scope showed continuing erratic activity from Kyle
Rivers's heart, violent surges dropping back to what might
be called valleys only to rise up again. The punishment his
body was enduring must have been massive.

"Carla, we will *have* to do something!'' Dr. Fowler exclaimed finally. "If Kyle is feeling anything at all right
now, if I concede for an instant that that is possible at this
stage, and isn't merely some kind of autonomous reflex,
Carla, it can only be pain, and judging by what we see,
massive pain at that.''

Any pretense at keeping his own emotions in check was
gone.

"Can't you see that?'' he begged. "Do you want him to
suffer like this? I can't believe that you do.''

"Are you saying that you will have to put Kyle out of
his misery?'' she demanded. "I thought you had already
pronounced him dead.''

"He *is* dead, I mean, it seemed that he was but now—''

"Then how can he be *feeling* anything at all? Yet, Dr.
Fowler, you told me it can only be pain.''

"If he's still alive, but that is a huge if. Clinically, Kyle
Rivers *must* be dead.''

"Look at all that activity on your machine. Is that the

way a dead man's body acts? Is it? Tell me, Dr. Fowler, tell me now.''

''But—?''

''But what?'' Carla interrupted. ''You *can* be wrong, isn't that it? He might not be dead after all!''

Dr. Fowler was frustrated, wanting to give Carla some hope but hoping to avoid anything that was false.

''I just don't know,'' he told her. ''The scope—''

He gasped as he gestured toward the round screen.

''What in the—?'' he started to speak, but simply sputtered without saying anything else momentarily, as he saw that the flat-line signal was no longer steady, but, rather, it was reacting in a less erratic fashion, the motions fluid instead.

''Doctor!'' a nurse spoke.

''Yes, I see it. I'm not blind, nurse, or stupid.''

The movements on the scope were close to text-book normal.

Suddenly, the fingers of Kyle's right hand closed weakly around Carla's wrist, and she could just barely hear him whisper, *''Dearest...Carla...I couldn't...leave you yet.''*

Carla was allowed the use of a bed in an empty room at the hospital, and her need to be awake to learn instantly any new development with Kyle gave way to her body's utter exhaustion, and she fell asleep as soon as her head touched the pillow.

Roxie decided to stay but Irving needed to get back to the house because he was hypoglycemic and needed rest more than she did.

Rocco Gilardi had been waiting in the visitors' lounge ever since they arrived at Nashville Memorial. But he wasn't aggravated.

''You aren't?'' Irving asked.

''With some celebrities, yes,'' the man told him. ''But

not Carla Gearhart. I know how serious it must be for her to behave like this.''

"Why don't you stay at her house for a couple of hours at least. Get a little sleep, and then come back.''

"That would be very nice.''

"I'm not taking over or anything,'' Irving assured him self-consciously. "Just trying to help a friend.''

"Mr. Chicolte?'' Gilardi spoke.

"Yes, young man?''

"She thinks a great deal of you. I don't know if she would be happy that I told you but I figure that you need as much encouragement as you can get since she will need to lean on you a lot until Mr. Rivers gets better.''

"I don't think he will.''

"Forgive me, sir, for contradicting you at a time like this but, you see, God isn't through with him yet.''

Irving did his best to suppress a sneer.

"If God can use Kyle Rivers, then why is God putting the poor guy through all this suffering?''

"Could we talk about it on the way home, sir?''

"I would be glad to do that, but I must warn you that I will not be at all receptive but, rather, blatantly antagonistic.''

Gilardi smiled as he said, "Some people feel I should have been a priest.''

"You must want to hear my confession, young man,'' Irving spoke facetiously.

"Whatever you need to talk about, sir.''

Irving smiled though he didn't really intend to do that.

"What is your name?'' he asked.

"Rocco, sir.''

Irving Chicolte hated admitting it to himself but there was something about this young driver that he was sure would make the trip back to Carla's home considerably more interesting than he could have anticipated a moment earlier.

Roxie was also given a vacant room at the hospital, though it was made clear that no guarantee was being made that she and Carla could be accommodated that way during each successive evening.

Carla did more pacing of corridors than any real sleeping. Part of the time she spent in Kyle's room, waiting for him to regain consciousness, but then she was advised that nurses and doctors would have to come and go through whatever was left of the night, in order to monitor his condition, and it would be difficult for her to get the kind of sleep she would need to conserve her strength.

But she was tense, always anticipating yet another frantic call, given the changing nature of Kyle's condition. And so she would take to walking that entire floor, which allowed Carla to see a kind of kaleidoscope of suffering, people with heart conditions, those who had just undergone major surgery, some with cancer, but there was one patient in particular who fascinated and frightened her.

A woman who had attempted suicide.

Carla asked a nurse about her. At first, the nurse was reluctant to disclose any personal information about her patient. But Carla's genuine interest and sympathy finally wore her down.

"We would have put her in a different section of the hospital except for the fact that it's jam-packed."

"Psychiatric cases?"

"That's right."

"Any idea why she tried to kill herself?"

The nurse, the oldest one on the staff, told her, "She claimed that she couldn't stand the loneliness."

"She had no one at all?"

"Her parents are dead. She never married. She seems to

have no friends of either sex. She lives alone in an apartment.''

''What does this woman do for a living?''

''She's an award-winning writer, Miss Gearhart. Her royalty earnings have been keeping her going, as far as we can tell. She could be enjoying a really fruitful life, a fulfilling one by anybody's measurement, for her works continue to be in much demand, and she's always receiving invitations for conversations, autograph parties, dinners with publishers, and so on. But she turns them all down.''

The nurse smiled sheepishly.

''When she was first brought in, she was ranting about many things. What I just told you is part of what we were able to get out of all that blathering.''

''How sad!''

''Truly sad, yes. I think I could stand anything in life except being alone, feeling isolated as she does. That would make *me* start thinking of a way out.''

''When Kyle gets stronger, I wonder if I could bring the two of them together. With his personality, he could do a great deal to encourage her.''

''That would be wonderful,'' the nurse agreed with some enthusiasm, ''but I doubt that it will ever happen.''

''Why do you say that?''

''Because she is too far gone. We all suspect that someday she will probably succeed in what she desperately wants.''

''Taking her own life? Is there *nothing* you can do?''

Carla had touched upon a subject that was a hot-button issue for this nurse.

''What can we hope for these days? The fact that suicide is becoming less and less a forbidden subject gives you some idea of why more and more people are doing it.''

She heard Roxie's voice coming from the room, and hesitated.

"It's awkward for me to do this," her friend was saying. "I don't believe in your God or any God, for that matter. But you do, I can see, and you got Carla to go along with you, and that's fine."

Roxie paused, and it seemed to Carla that she was dealing with emotions that had not surfaced in a very long time.

"I always thought the God of the Jews was vengeful and angry, and the Christian God was cold and distant and, more than likely, ineffectual letting people suffer needlessly. Since I couldn't accept either, I decided that I would live as though there were no one up there in the sky, that we were truly alone in this world, and we had to fight hard to survive, with no divine help ever coming.

"But then I heard your concert just last night. How long ago that seems, Kyle! You convinced me of the depth of *your* faith. You got through to this callous, bitter, unbelieving broad! And that's no mean feat. I could never take the plunge but you obviously had, and your faith had changed your life as well as Carla's.

"But now look at what has happened to you! Is that the work of a loving God? I think not. I'll repeat that, Kyle, *I* think not. But I hope that if you pull through, you do not lose *your* beliefs, and that Carla never wavers, either.

"We need an anchor in this world, and that's what scares me. I have none. I just get through each day on my own strength, and yet there are times when I feel so weak, so unable to rejoin the rat race.

"And now something's happened that I can't fight. I am dying. My cancer is the slow kind. It will give me a few years maybe but then that is it. I go to the grave with no hope. Can you imagine how awful it is to know that you are dying and when you believe there's nothing more, that you will just disappear, as though you've never existed?

"Kyle, if you can hear me, pray to this supposedly merciful God of yours that He gives you some more time, though I imagine that you've already been doing that. Do it again, though, for Carla's sake. Your death anytime soon would utterly destroy that woman. I don't want her to become like me. I can't see this vibrant, beautiful, happy individual ending up like a bad copy of Roxie Chicolte."

She paused, and then added, "I would like to attend your wedding. Isn't *that* something? It'll probably be in a church. Isn't that something? I don't even go to a synagogue, haven't for a long time!

"I can't say anything else. I am tired. Carla will tell you everything, I am sure. You are a wonderful young man. If anybody could convert me, it would be you. But don't worry about this old bag. Pray that your God gives you back to Carla, and that the two of you have a long, happy life together."

Carla peeked in past the slightly ajar door. She saw Roxie leaning over and kissing Kyle on the forehead.

"It would have been so fine to have a son like you," her friend whispered.

And then she was headed for the door.

Carla stepped back, as far down the corridor as she could get before Roxie stepped into it.

"Your Kyle is speaking to God right now, I think," she said. "Let me know what happens."

"Are you leaving already?" Carla asked.

"Here, yes, and Nashville, yes. My husband and I have a business to attend to, you know."

"But, Roxie, what if Kyle—?"

Carla saw Roxie's hand clench, as if fighting the urge to slap her.

"Don't you *dare* say that!" she spoke. "Don't even think it! He is strong, and he loves you, and he—"

She threw her head back as tears filled her eyes.

"—and he has faith, *real* faith. It's something to hold

on to, Carla. It's something to keep you both going. You may not realize how fortunate you are to have it!''

"You're right, Roxie. I'm just so afraid." Tears threatened once more, but Carla fought to hold them back. "I just have to hold on, for Kyle. I know if I were the one in that hospital bed, his trust in the Lord wouldn't waver for a moment."

Roxie reached out and patted Carla's arm. "You'd better hurry back to Kyle, stay with him every minute. I'll be there as soon as I can."

"Bless you," Carla told her. "I guess I'll have to renew my contract with the agency now," she joked.

"And there goes my return home in the morning!" Roxie said, throwing her hands up in mock frustration.

Carla dashed out of the visitor's room and hurried back to Kyle's room. When she entered, he was sitting up in bed and smiling at her.

"Let me kiss you...before I pass out again...." he said, his voice very weak. "Grab the moment...babe."

Kyle had little strength but at least he was conscious, and could talk with coherence though Carla wondered how long that would last. His weakness worried her, yet she hadn't lost sight of how much of a miracle his very survival was.

"Carla..." he muttered, his voice thick. "I think I can hold on this time. I can hardly move but I don't feel as though I am going to pass out anytime soon."

She was holding his hand, treasuring the moment and realizing again how close she'd come to losing him.

"Did you hear Roxie a little while ago?" she asked.

"I remember a voice. A few words here and there. Seemed like it was very far away. Was that Roxie?"

"It was. And she was sitting where I am now. She talked in a way I have never known she was capable of."

"That woman's searching whether she admits it or not."

"But, Kyle, she was talking about *your* relationship with God."

"I think her own was tucked in with it. Talking about me was the easiest way she had of getting into it."

He paused, grunting a bit.

"Pain?" Carla asked apprehensively.

"No, just thinking. She was willing to concede that God was real for me, but that He didn't exist for her."

"And she was telling you how much you are needed, as well as how deeply you are loved."

"Now that would have been nice to hear."

"I wonder if God actually considered what Roxie was saying a kind of prayer?" Carla mused.

"I have no idea except that Scripture says about God using even the most broken of vessels."

Carla touched her lips with her middle fingers.

"I never thought of her that way."

"But God did, Carla, before Roxie Chicolte was ever born."

"You believe that? That He had her in His mind, to create her before she was a fetus? Is that possible?"

Kyle chuckled though it hurt him a bit to do so.

"You're asking if something like that is possible for God?"

She realized what she had said and added, "But she must be a disappointment to Him then. Look at how she has lived her life until now. You would be startled if you knew just some of the sins she's committed."

"God doesn't say after sin number forty-seven or one hundred or one thousand that He's going to turn His back on anyone. God never gives up on us. Even if we give up on Him. And look at Roxie," he added, "here she is, saying what might have come pretty close to a prayer!" Kyle exclaimed, the irony obvious.

"Remember, though, that she was actually talking to you."

"Not God?"

"Not as far as she was concerned."

"But God heard it. That's what matters."

Carla smiled as she looked at Kyle.

"Did I say something funny?" he asked.

"I'm just enjoying what I thought I might never be able to do again."

"What's that?"

"Listening to your voice. Looking at your face. Imagining what it would be like about now to give you the longest, sweetest kiss ever!

"You don't have to wait any longer, not on my account. But you'll have to do most of the work. I'm not able to do any moving around yet. At least I'm not numb all over!"

That was all she needed to hear.

Carla fell asleep in the chair next to Kyle's bed, though she would awaken every so often and glance at him, see that he seemed to be sleeping without discomfort, and then doze off again.

He looks as though nothing has happened, she thought during one of those fleeting periods of being awake. *There's even a little smile on his face.*

She reached over and touched his arm then.

How could I be loving you so much? she asked herself. *But I do, oh, man, I do. I love touching you. Before yesterday, I could hardly stand it when we weren't together, when I couldn't feel your arms around me. How strong you are, Kyle! You could pick me up and throw me over your back and walk away, and I wouldn't scream, 'Let me down! Let me down!' Because I wouldn't care where you were going. As long as you were taking me with you, I would go without protest.*

She chuckled to herself.

I've painted a picture of you as some kind of modern caveman. But you're not like that at all. You consider me first before you think about yourself. You—

Kyle's head turned in her direction, his eyes closed, his lips parted slightly.

I want so much to kiss you again and again right now, just like a few minutes ago. But you need your rest, beloved. There'll be plenty of time later, plenty—

She surrendered once more to sleep, a smile on her own face.

Something remarkable happened the morning Kyle was released from Nashville Memorial....

After spending three hours a day for an entire month in the rehab center of the hospital, Kyle Rivers had gotten back much of his strength but not all of it. So, a wheelchair was brought to his room as a precaution.

"I don't want that, Carla!' he declared unequivocally as it was wheeled in by an intern. "It's too embarrassing. I'm not a cripple now."

"There's no other way," Carla told him just as firmly, narrowing her eyes for emphasis. "What if you fall?"

"If I fall, I'll just stand up again," he remarked matter-of-factly. "Isn't it as simple as that?"

"No, Kyle, it's not that simple at all, not in a million years, my love!"

"This isn't like you, Carla," he observed, sounding disgruntled.

Carla had seen Kyle's obtuse side before but it hadn't really bothered her very much until now.

"I'm trying to protect you," she said, exasperated.

"It seems more like you're trying to mother me."

As soon as Kyle had spoken, he hated what he had said, worried that Carla would take it as an oblique reference to the age difference between them when he had meant it only figuratively.

But she was not going to be distracted by that or anything else that Kyle might have to say.

"But what if you *do* hurt yourself?" she demanded.

"It'll never happen, Carla," he replied, a certain smile crossing his face that he knew usually made her become little more than putty in his hands.

However, Carla, steeling herself, determined that he would be the one to cave in this time.

"You can't be sure of that," she argued, armed with what the doctors had told her about his condition. "Is it worth the kind of chance you'd be taking?"

"Who knows? But I *can* be sure of something else."

"What's that, Kyle?" Carla asked, not accustomed to the stubborn streak he was revealing.

"It's something I *need* to do. I need to *walk* out of here. I'm not an invalid, and I don't want to be carted out like one."

Carla hesitated, torn between the caution that had been embodied in the expert medical opinions she had received just a couple of days before, and what was obviously of supreme importance to Kyle.

How can I be telling him what to do? she thought. *Ordering my future husband around as though he is my helpless child instead?*

It was proving awkward for Carla to feel that Kyle was having to depend upon her so completely when part of the personal fantasy she had built up in her mind as their romance was developing happened to be how much she could lean on *him* as time passed, happily giving up a sizable chunk of her independence in return for the reassuring presence of a man as strong as he was.

Kyle was in bed and she sat down next to him, taking hold of his hand.

"Do you know how much I love you?" she asked. "Do you know how completely your soul and mine have become intertwined?"

That fact alone was initially perplexing to Carla. Her independence had been so important to her that her need for it had destroyed most of her earlier relationships with men. And yet this mattered less and less as her feelings for Kyle mushroomed.

"Probably as much as it is with me, though I don't see how that's possible," he said straightforwardly. "I would do anything for you, my love. If by dying that meant you would live, I'd never hesitate, not for a single second."

He was frowning as he added, "But, Carla, please, I beg you to do this for me. Is it so much to ask?"

She tried to sound more severe than she actually felt.

"It *is* too much, Kyle," she told him flatly, hating the wounded expression that danced across his irresistible young face. "And I'll tell you exactly why. Because if it's too much strain on your system, if something does go wrong, and you wind up back in this hospital or maybe never leave it in the first place, yes, *that* is far, far too much to ask of me just to satisfy some whim of yours."

"Is that what you think this is all about?" he asked.

"No, that isn't all, Kyle. There's more to it, something else involved that, if you were really looking at this situation realistically, you'd see why what you want is so wrongheaded."

Kyle was frowning, trying to get a handle on what she was saying.

"I don't know what you're getting at," he acknowledged.

"Pride."

He started to object but she raised her hand and shot him a glance that was unmistakable.

"That's all it amounts to, my love, simple pride. Remember what Scripture says: 'Pride goes before a fall.' You don't want anyone to pity you. You want to seem as strong, as resilient, as macho as people seem to think you are.

"Yet is it so unmanly, Kyle, to acknowledge that you have been close to death, that your body is weakened as a result, and you'll need time to get back to the way you were before the accident?"

Kyle looked at her, grinned, and asked, "Is this the way you're going to act after we are married?"

"You'd better believe it!"

"Praise God!" he said as he leaned over and kissed her.

"So is it the wheelchair or not?" she asked.

"What are you waiting for?" he said, a slight blush on his cheeks.

Chapter Ten

Resigned to the wheelchair, and also the necessity of having an intern push it instead of Carla doing this, Kyle swallowed hard as the elevator stopped at the ground floor.

What's going to be happening next? he wondered. The doors slid open, and, immediately, electronic flashes went off in rapid succession, nearly a dozen reporters and photographers standing in the corridor outside.

"This was what I was hoping to avoid," he whispered.

"It's the deck you've been dealt," Carla replied sympathetically. "We'll get through this, trust me."

He smiled sweetly and gritted his teeth as the wheelchair was pushed through that little group, and he headed toward the front exit.

Only to encounter another gathering, including the hospital's chief of staff Dr. Lance Mayfield and the esteemed neurological specialist, Dr. Andros Gregaris, as well as nearly a dozen nurses, interns and some patients.

"You are a remarkable young man," Gregaris told him. "I was prepared not to like you. At first I even detested you. But now I would be pleased to adopt you."

Several people chuckled at that since it revealed a softer side of this Spartan-seeming Greek that they would have bet just did not exist.

Mayfield spoke up then.

"What my colleague is saying," he commented, "is that you are remarkable because of a stunning recovery and yet that isn't the only reason. Look at what you've done to help other patients. I've never seen anything like it."

During the three weeks Kyle was confined to Nashville Memorial, he had had occasion to visit with a number of other men and women who were in the midst of one health crisis or another. Some would come to him. And, also, he would go to them after he had regained enough strength, with Carla or an intern helping him.

"I've never been to a hospital before now," Kyle told her at one point. "Isn't that amazing when you think of it?"

"Are you kidding?" Carla asked, not quite sure whether he was being facetious.

"I'm really serious," he told her earnestly. "Nobody in our family has ever gone. I never had to visit ailing friends in the hospital. I guess I've been shielded from a lot of things in my life."

"You can say that again!"

"Then I look around and think about the other patients here."

"What about them?"

"Some are completely alone, Carla. Imagine that, will you? How sad to think of it! Here I am, with so much— you, students from the college coming in to see me, all the get well cards, flowers, you know. I could never feel alone, rejected because the Lord has provided so abundantly.

"Yet there are half a dozen hurting folks here who have never received any of that. Nobody visits them at all. Oh, Carla, they were so glad to have you and me, and not just a nurse or a doctor stop in, say hello and spend a few minutes.

"I've asked the nurses to pass out all the flowers I've received, concentrating on those patients I listed on a sheet of paper this morning. I don't think anybody who gave them to me will mind."

"I agree," she replied, "and I'm sure they won't even be surprised that you've gone and done this."

"Bless you, Carla."

"You've got a gift, Kyle. There's a magic something or other about you that people would have to be blind not to notice."

"Magic? You know I don't believe in that sort of thing."

"I was talking figuratively. My, are you touchy today!"

"I guess I am," he admitted.

"Mind telling me why? Is it all this time you've spent here in Nashville Memorial? That would make *me* irritable!"

He shrugged his shoulders. "I don't have my thoughts together yet. It's probably nothing at all, Carla," he told her. "Why not give me some space on this, okay?"

"Fine," she said, feeling perturbed, and more than a little apprehensive at the change in his attitude.

Kyle saw her expression.

"Forgive me for this," he asked.

"Naturally. But I'm anxious to know when *anything's* bothering you. If that makes me nosy, I've got to plead guilty."

"And I think the same way about you," Kyle said, his voice huskier.

Her own manner softened as she said, "Why don't we let it go until you feel you want to say something?"

Kyle was relieved.

"That'd be great," he agreed.

"Kyle?"

"Yes, Carla?"

"I love you with my mind, body and soul," she told him, her heart beating faster as she spoke.

"Just as I love you, Carla. I can't wait until we're married," Kyle whispered as his hand tightened around her own, which made her heart go into racing mode.

As soon as an intern had taken the wheelchair outside, Rocco Gilardi backed up the Bentley a bit, then helped get Kyle into the back seat.

"There will be help at your house, Miss Gearhart," the driver told her.

"Thank you so much," Carla replied, then walked around the back of the car and got in next to Kyle from the opposite side.

"It's over," he said, sounding very tired, his muscles hurting from the strain of the past few weeks. "How quickly my life changed."

"Are you going after that lousy drunken driver who caused all this?" Carla asked reasonably, hoping that he would say yes, and yet not completely surprised by the answer he did give.

"No..." he spoke simply.

"Why not?"

"Because the police have thrown him in jail, fined him, and the DMV revoked his license."

Carla thought Kyle had a tendency to be too soft in certain matters, too slow to anger even when some heat seemed necessary.

"Does that satisfy you?" Carla asked skeptically. "I have to admit that it would do very little to appease me, frankly."

And Kyle, for his part, thought he detected a propensity in Carla to fly off the handle far too easily.

"But why, Carla?" he probed with some concern. "The

man is ruined for the foreseeable future. The aftermath will probably stay with him for the rest of his life. Isn't that punishment enough?''

"You could have died," she stated the obvious. "Need I say anything else, Kyle? Surely that prospect is enough to make you want to cause *him* some genuine pain? At the very least, see him pay financially for the grief he's caused us?"

"I don't feel that need Carla, certainly not to the extent that you do."

"I can't believe you're saying this, after what you've gone through and God knows what's ahead for you."

"What you seem to want sounds a lot like vengeance," he told her.

"But it's natural for someone to feel like I do. It's what I would expect of *you* more than anyone."

"Acting naturally, as you call it, can mean acting sinfully, Carla. The natural person is inherently at odds with God. There is too much that I already do *naturally* that is offensive to Him. Why knowingly add to the list?"

"You're sounding more and more like a preacher."

"Is that so bad?"

"Of course not. It's just that—"

He interrupted her by repeating her name a couple of times, with a touch of condescension, then said, "Listen, I know what's really wrong."

"Oh, you read minds now," Carla remarked sarcastically. "Is that another gift of the Spirit that you possess?"

"Please, Carla, listen to me, okay?"

"All right, I'll listen."

"You're still wondering what I meant when I hinted earlier that something was bothering me, isn't that it?"

Carla hadn't realized that she'd come across so transparently.

"Right…" she acknowledged, hating to have to do that but her honesty leaving her no choice.

Kyle noticed the real apprehension on her face, and felt sorry about having raised the subject.

"Can we wait until we get back to the house?" he asked, hoping to have some time either to think of what to say or, perhaps, letting the matter drop altogether.

"Yes, we can," she told him.

The way Carla replied showed how she really felt.

In a short period of time, Kyle had come to be able to read her as well as someone who had been married to his wife a number of years.

"But you'd like to get it off your mind now?" he added. "Am I right?"

Carla had to admit that he was hitting bull's-eyes.

"I would be lying if I said otherwise," she acknowledged.

"All right," he told her, "I'll do my best."

"Now?"

"Now."

Carla braced herself emotionally, praying that nothing serious was about to disrupt their relationship.

"Carla, back there at the hospital…" Kyle said slowly, choosing every word with special care.

"Yes…"

"You acted differently, you know."

"How differently?"

"It's hard to describe. You were just not yourself."

"It *was* me yet I wasn't myself. Now *that* sounds pretty strange," she said, chuckling, trying to lighten the moment.

"You seemed totally in control."

She almost choked on that one.

"I *seemed* in control?" she repeated. "That sounds like an accusation the way you say it, Kyle."

Carla hated herself for succumbing to some anger but

that was exactly what she did as she went on to say, "You mean, don't you, that a good woman is someone who is shy and retiring, and has learned *never* to assert herself too authoritatively in a man's world. Is that the way you look at it?"

Kyle was frowning, increasingly regretting that moment.

"Let's not talk anymore, not like this," he suggested evasively. "We need to cool down. Our emotions have been dealt some heavy blows over the past four weeks."

Carla was going to say something else but decided not to, since Kyle was starting to sound more and more weary, and she had to weigh everything against its impact on his physical condition.

So, they rode mostly in silence the rest of the way except for an occasional comment that amounted to chitchat, nothing more...with one exception.

The route Gilardi chose was something of a shortcut, using local roads rather than the main highway, taking them past the church Carla had started to attend not long before Kyle entered her life.

"I was feeling the need for something more in my life a few months ago...." she told him. "After nearly a decade in country music, enduring the many one-nighters, the traveling from town to town, even though later I had my own air-conditioned bus, I was close to becoming burnt out."

"When you've got, say, a dozen gigs in two weeks, how do you get up before an audience and appear fresh each matinee or night?" Kyle asked. "When I'm doing a weekend at just one place, three performances all told, by the time I finish the last one, I'm starting to feel it, Carla."

"Even at *your* age," she said, grinning.

"Why, that's right! How in the world do you get through it at yours?"

And then they both burst out laughing.

"You know, Kyle," she said after they had stopped, "it's not hard to understand what happened to Elvis."

"I've had a burden about him for a long time," he said.

"I didn't know that."

"I sure have. The man read the Bible, went to church, prayed, confessed his faith, yet ended up the way he did."

"He should still be alive today."

"He isn't?" Kyle asked with mock surprise.

"If Elvis is alive, then I had dinner with Hank Williams Sr. last night!"

"And Patsy Cline stopped by to say hello."

They looked at one another and felt uncomfortable at the same time.

"We shouldn't be kidding like this," Kyle said apologetically. "They all died so tragically."

"And *how* they died scares the living daylights out of me."

"You worry about a plane crash?"

"Absolutely, Kyle. I do fifty thousand air miles a year, The odds go more and more against me with each new flight. Until you came along, I wondered if I would start doing the drug thing, too."

He placed his fingers on the back of her hand and patted her gently.

"That will never happen, my love."

"Not too long ago, I might not have been able to agree with you," Carla said, a haunted expression on her face.

"But your life is very different now," he reminded her. "You have me to reach out to when you're feeling low, and more importantly, you have the Lord."

"Yes, that's true." Carla smiled and squeezed his hand.

Kyle frowned suddenly, and touched his temple with the middle fingers of his left hand.

"Are you all right?" she asked.

"Just a sudden headache."

"This has been too intense," Carla reasoned.

"Maybe so..."

They did not talk further, while Carla spent the last twenty minutes of the ride home battling emotions that were clearly overreacting to that brief little indication of Kyle's discomfort, magnifying it into something more ominous.

As soon as they arrived, Gilardi summoned Carla's butler and the two of them helped get Kyle to the guest quarters on the first floor since there was no way he could be safely taken upstairs.

Afterward, as Carla pulled the covers over him, he looked up at her and whispered, "I don't know what I've been saying. I'm sure not thinking as I should be. I guess it's everything coming back on me, the accident, the pain, dying. *Oh, Carla, dying...*"

His expression was desperate.

"Seeing you fading away as my life seemed to be flowing out of my body, I wanted to reach out and hold you and take you with me because I didn't want to be alone. How awful to die like that, how—"

She kissed him on the forehead.

"Shush..." she said with a tenderness that seemed to be felt in every inch of her body. "This, too, shall pass."

"It will, won't it, Carla, it surely will," he replied, trying to keep his eyes open, wanting to see her like that, that once-a-stranger's face now so familiar, every wrinkle, every inch of her nose and cheeks and that rather pointed chin.

She paused, and saw that he was still looking at her.

"Rest now, love," she said.

She had nearly shut the door when, as an afterthought, she opened it again, and added, "Kyle?"

"Yes...Carla...?" his weak voice spoke.

"I wanted to go with you back there," she told him. "Nobody would have had to drag me, kicking and screaming, you know. If I could have died with you, I would have given up everything to do that because living without you wouldn't have been life at all. I couldn't bear not doing *everything* to keep you with me."

"Blessed Carla..." he muttered.

"Don't call me that," she told him. "You're deceiving yourself. I am far less than blessed, as you have just seen."

"Not to me," Kyle said. "Not to me, dear Carla. You are everything I could ever want or need. Loving you will be what I do for the rest of my life."

She nearly went back into the bedroom, feeling the need to sit beside him for a few minutes but she restrained herself.

"Rest well, my love," she whispered, throwing him a kiss.

"I will," he said so softly that she had to strain to hear. "Angels abide..."

A tear trickled down Kyle's cheek as he closed his eyes, and slept.

Chapter Eleven

The benefits of a certain wealth...

Carla loved to sit on the rolling front lawn of her extensive property, and look at the ageless Spanish moss hanging from the old oak trees that were found in abundance on her land, unusual for that region, since that feathery growth was usually found in Louisiana, particularly near New Orleans.

"It looks kind of unreal as dusk comes, and the rays of a dying sun touch it," she told Kyle when he first visited, which was about a week after they'd met. "I never get tired of looking, of breathing in the air scented with the fragrance of my roses or my lilacs."

"You speak like a poet," he told her, "and a dreamer."

"The lyrics of a good song are poetry," Carla stated. "That makes me a singing poet, I guess. And what creative person is not something of a dreamer, impatient with reality as it exists."

"Do you write many of your songs?"

"I didn't at the beginning. It was so much easier to get

permission to use someone else's. Writing music is *very* hard work.''

He nodded in agreement.

''So is a relationship, a tough, tough business,'' he said. ''So many students at my college come from broken homes.''

Carla picked up on those few words.

''Any serious doubts about *us* making it work?''

''None.''

''Yet you're obviously thinking about those who fail.''

''I guess it's all so unreal to me.''

''That you and I would be dating?''

''Carla, you are the biggest female star country music has ever seen. And I am a nobody. Yet here we are.''

''Don't you ever say that!'' she admonished him. ''I want you to promise that you never will again.''

''That we're dating?''

''No, dummy! That you're a nobody.''

''But that's the way I feel sometimes.''

''Why, Kyle? You're the wisest, most talented, most loving man I have ever met. Not to mention the handsomest,'' she added. ''Before I met you, I was so caught up in judging a person's worth by the outside—by their money, or fame or a fancy title. But now I see none of that matters. Only the quality of their heart and spirit.''

They stopped talking as they watched a new sunset's gold-red rays beaming through the Spanish moss.

''Man, I see what you mean!'' Kyle exclaimed, his eyes wide-open. ''It's really beautiful.''

''If I'm tense, I just lie back on the grass, as you and I are doing, and look up, and sigh and thank God for what I have.''

''I thank God I have you in my life, Carla. And I want us to be married. Soon,'' he insisted. He reached over and squeezed her hand. "Each day, it gets more difficult to wait to make you mine."

"For me, too. Sometimes I think, what's the difference if we do make love before we get married? Just look at the tabloids, or any of those entertainment news shows on TV. Everyone in the world thinks…"

"But that's just the point, sweetheart," Kyle interrupted. "What other people think or say about us doesn't matter. The Bible *says* marriage before sex and parenthood, Carla. There are no exceptions."

"That's so hard. People have emotions. Emotions can't always be controlled, especially in an intimate situation."

"It is hard, Carla. But have you and I become second-class human beings because we're waiting?"

"No, we haven't, but—"

He leaned over and nibbled at her ear.

"Think of the peace of mind we'll have on our honeymoon."

Despite the candor of that moment, despite the love that existed between them, Carla was to discover later that evening that the two of them would face a turning point in their relationship.

The more Carla learned about Kyle's views on a variety of subjects the more she worried about their very different points of view on important issues. She had grown up with sharply formed opinions on abortion, welfare and other subjects, and not voicing them would have seemed dishonest and hypocritical to her.

So, she decided to confront him.

Kyle kept staring at her, and never interrupted. Even after she was finished, and waited for a response, he said nothing right away but sat back, looking a little like a cow chewing its cud.

"Say something," she told him, irritated, wondering if she was seeing another side of him that was hardly endearing, one that treated her heartfelt convictions with a flippant attitude that bordered on contempt.

"I think you're wonderful," he replied finally, absolutely disarming her when she most expected to start a raging argument or debate with him.

"But we disagree on some heavy-duty subjects," she said, trying to justify the way she felt.

"Do you love me?" Kyle asked.

"Yes..."

"And I love you. Tell me, does *anything* else matter, Carla?"

She could give him only one answer.

"Nothing..." she admitted. "But is that *honestly* the way you feel? If I'm pro-choice, and you're pro-life, that's not enough to end our relationship?"

Kyle hesitated, and as far as Carla was concerned this said more than a library of books ever could.

They had been standing in the hallway just below a spiral staircase that was so common to Southern mansions.

"Enough!" she declared as she turned and hurried up the steps to her bedroom, slamming the door behind her.

Trembling, she fell down on the large canopied bed.

Does anything but my love for Kyle matter? she asked herself. *Should we let politics and the like divide us?*

Carla knew that the problem with her was that such subjects had been *causes* with her, and yet, despite the way Kyle felt, he never seemed especially *passionate* about his views.

I have earned the right to feel as I do, she thought. *I have been in the trenches. Kyle's in some ivory tower, not willing to sacrifice his time, his effort, his convenience!*

She brought her hand to her mouth, as she wondered how deep *anything* went as far as his outlook. Had he been so spoiled, gifted with his good looks and charm, and a natural intelligence, that he had never had to struggle for much in his life, perhaps in some areas regarding money, but nothing more than that.

"We are so different...." she murmured, "in age, in outlook, in—"

But there was no longer any difference between them in terms of their faith. Carla had never been an atheist but she had harbored a distrust of organized religion that had carried through virtually all of her adult life to date.

So much of a change in so short a time, she mused to herself. *He swept away all of my cynicism.*

He did not achieve this by initially spouting Bible verses but did so by his example: his kindness, his consistency, his low-key approach.

"When I was a kid, religion was shoved down my throat," she had told Kyle early on. "And I rejected it after awhile."

"Sometimes people have to find things on their own," he reasoned. "A decision you make because your parents practically *demand* it is not one that can be called really sincere. More than any other decision in life, the one that involves faith and worship and the Bible *must* be from the center of somebody's soul. God can look inside us. He knows whether we mean it or not."

Carla had leaned back against the headboard, trying to get a clear view of the way she was reacting, but not succeeding. After two previous marriages, both before she was thirty years old, she had developed a fear of ever making that kind of mistake again.

And so I'm going to drive away the one man who can make me happy, she told herself. *What good will my convictions be if I'm old and lonely and miserable?*

She hugged herself, shivering.

"Oh, God, help me!" she said out loud.

A few minutes passed.

She thought she heard the front door slammed shut.

"He's leaving!" she exclaimed. "What an idiot I am!"

And yet she still could not bring herself to hurry downstairs and race after him. Kyle had been very forceful defending his viewpoints while she took his words personally, as though he were insulting her and not simply disagreeing with her opinions.

That was it. It was over.

They weren't going to make it through this.

Knocking...

"May I come in?" Kyle asked.

She tried to appear as firm as before.

"I think we've said all we needed to," she declared.

He sat down on the edge of the bed.

"My love," he told her, "don't you understand that I respect the freedom you have to believe the way you want?"

All of Carla's carefully thought out reasons for ending their relationship were collapsing in just a few minutes but then she had discovered this was one of his gifts, getting through a tense situation and repairing feelings pretty quickly.

"Are you sure? You seemed to disagree with me pretty forcefully a few minutes ago."

"Yes, I did. And I'd do it again. But I've got no problem with you having convictions that are the *opposite* of mine! In fact, it means that you and I can look forward to having some really lively debates, without throwing in the towel on our relationship. That's wonderful, Carla! How many married couples have enough respect for one another's intelligence to find this sort of thing stimulating, even fun?"

He looked at her with an encouraging expression.

"Does this help, Carla?" he asked. "I pray that it does. I love you more than anything or anyone, except the Lord."

They embraced, Carla gasping silently as Kyle's muscular arms wrapped around her. She could feel the heat from his body, even sense the beating of his heart, and she knew, how truly she knew, whatever the extent to which she might disagree with him about one topic or another, only a moment such as that, their surroundings forgotten, the world no bigger than the tiny part of it that they occupied, could have any significance for them, for tomorrow and the day after that, for the rest of their lives.

Chapter Twelve

Angels abide...

As Carla went to sleep that night, wishing more than ever that Kyle was beside her, hating more than ever being alone, especially when he was right downstairs, she realized how forgiving her future husband was, bringing to mind a moment that she could not possibly forget for the rest of her life.

He knows that I have been married twice before, she thought, *and I have not hidden from him the fact that I have had a number of lovers over the years. I really am used merchandise. How I tried, early on, to persuade him that someone as decent as he deserved a younger, unspoiled woman as his life partner but he would not listen, would not allow me to stop a relationship that had been growing so fast that we scarcely had time to think about anything but getting married.*

But Kyle brushed aside all revelations about her past without expressing any surprise whatever.

"I know you're in show business," he said. "I have an idea of what goes on."

"And you still want me?" she asked, with a touch of cynicism. "How could you? I just don't understand how."

"Because the Lord brought us together, Carla."

"You can be so sure of that?"

"I don't know what He has planned for the two of us but that's where faith and trust come in, you know."

"If only I could be as sure as you are, if only I could feel as though—"

"It's forgiven," he interrupted her. "It's forgotten. That's the answer. Take ahold of it, hold it tight to you. Our faith stands or falls on forgiveness bestowed upon us by a holy God. Rejoice, Carla!"

"But you have no idea of all that I've done—"

"Quiet, Carla," he said, trying to avoid arrogance or any sense of his exerting macho dominance.

"But it's true. You can't pretend—"

"Nobody's pretending," Kyle interrupted again.

"Yes, you are. You're acting as though none of this happened."

"As far as I am concerned, it didn't."

"There! That's what I just told you. Pretending!"

"It's not pretense at all," he told her, showing as much patience as he could muster. "When God forgives our sin, He isn't pretending. As far as He is concerned, none of it exists. It's been washed away."

"But you said that we sin every day."

"We do."

"And God forgives us every day, Kyle?"

She found that hard, almost fatally hard to accept, though she desperately *wanted* to believe it.

"If only I could feel that you are right," she mused, "if only I could grab hold of it and let it become a part of me."

"Read your Bible," he urged her. "It's all there."

And read she did, chapter after chapter, day after day,

absorbing every bit as much as she could, and then peppering Kyle with all sorts of questions about what seemed to her to be difficult passages. Before long, as he explained what she needed to know, she was able to find some common ground with him, and some sense of security that he was correct in what he had been telling her.

"If only I could feel the peace you talk about," she said, trembling at the possibility of being able to come to grips with her past, and not feel like a common whore, for she had been with enough men to earn her that description.

"It's called the peace that passes understanding because, from a human point of view, it seems impossible. Even a murderer can gain forgiveness. There are no limitations, Carla, because God does not limit Himself."

"Before I met you, none of it mattered, the adulterous relationships, the infidelities, the one-night stands. I even kept some sort of mental scorecard, Kyle. Now all of that has come back to haunt me. And I feel dirty."

Ironically they were in the spa at one end of Carla's indoor heated swimming pool.

He gently closed his hands around her shoulders.

"That's where our faith comes in," he assured her. "We *know* by faith that God forgives us."

"But even if he does forgive my past, what about the present? Will I always face temptation? Do you?"

"Don't you think that I feel tempted, the same as you do, Carla?" he told her. "Sometimes it takes all my willpower to resist. But think of this, think of how we please God when we are successful, and the things of the spirit win out over the things of the flesh."

"If only you weren't the most attractive man I've ever met."

And Carla had "known" several who could have claimed that identification, men who were marketed as the "flavor of the month," their popularity lasting for a year or two and then fading.

"I could try not to be," he said, looking like a shy over-size boy. "I could look like I needed a shave."

"No!" Carla exclaimed. "That would make matters worse. A rougher, unkempt image, I...I couldn't stand. Worse yet, I couldn't resist—"

He smiled, and she had to close her eyes for a moment because Kyle's charm was at its most devastating then.

"I could wear a tie all the time instead of an open shirt," he told her. "An ugly tie," he added.

"Well, that *would* help," she replied, opening her eyes.

They stopped talking for a while, and lay back in the spa, and looked up at the stars through the transparent sky-light.

"Looking up there, I think of the vastness of what God has created, and how little this planet seems in the overall scheme of things, and, yes, oh, yes, how insignificant you and I would be if it weren't for His love for us, His recognition that we are not worthless at all but that we matter greatly to Him."

"Is that where we will go when we die?" she asked.

"All the old allegories, the symbols, the rest suggest it is, but no one can truly say for sure."

"Will we be floating in space between those stars?"

He laughed rather heartily, and she felt embarrassed, wondering if he was making fun of her lack of knowledge about such matters.

"Are you mocking me?" Carla asked.

"No, no, it's just a funny idea. Jesus talks about many mansions, and some folks are bound to think that He meant the thousands upon thousands of planets, but I don't go along with that."

"Well, what do you think heaven will be like?"

"Great joy," he told her. "Reunion with loved ones who have gone on ahead of us."

"Kyle..." she spoke musingly.

"Another tough question?" he replied, not minding at all, since he enjoyed the role of being a kind of spiritual tutor.

"Maybe so," Carla said.

"Let it rip," he commented.

Carla cleared her throat.

"Animals..." she spoke, finally bringing up a subject that she had been hoping Kyle could address.

"What about them?" he asked.

"I mean, do you have any idea if pets go to heaven?"

"Carla, I'm not a theologian, you know."

"Yes, I know, but, after all, you understand more than I do."

"Even so..."

"All right, then, tell me what you can. Your opinion, your hunch, your feeling, whatever? Do pets go to heaven?"

"I think so, actually," he admitted.

"Tell me why you feel that way."

"Because God has created them as friends for us. They give us unconditional love. And they bring out the same in us."

"I know what you mean. I've not had a cat for a few years. And the house seems lonelier without at least one."

"That's how I feel. Unfortunately, my landlord won't allow any of the tenants to have pets."

"All right, then, *why* did you think pets go to heaven?"

"Because something as wonderful as a devoted dog, for example, who saves a family from being trapped by fire—and cats do that, too—I just can't see how God would allow it to expire at the end of its life.

"As far as I can see, that wouldn't be righteous or kind

or loving. Could I believe in a God who would just wipe out something as devoted and valiant as that dog? It would be very difficult for me, Carla.''

She leaned her head on his bare shoulder. "Do you want a dog?" she asked.

He had a prankish smile on his face as he replied, "After we move into my apartment? I told you my landlord won't—"

"What?" she shouted, interrupting him.

"I know it's only three small rooms," he said, rolling his eyes in an exaggerated manner. "I could redecorate it with some expensive things that I went ahead and bought with your money, and you'd feel right at home, I'm sure, but we'd have to forget about pets unfortunately, unless you bribed the landlord.''

"And what would we do with this place?" she asked.

"Oh, rent it out for a tidy sum, I suspect," he said with a laugh.

Even as he spoke, he felt the joyous freedom of being able to joke with Carla on that level.

Lord, he thought, *I feel so happy with this woman. Thank you for bringing her into my life.*

Carla's eyes were becoming even wider, her cheeks reddening, but then Kyle began laughing uncontrollably as he said, *"Gotcha!"*

"Your time will come!" she laughed good-naturedly as they collapsed into one another's arms.

After spending a night asleep or sitting up in bed, her mind awash with memories of the weeks of their relationship before the accident, Carla looked at herself in the mirror on her makeup table.

"Do you realize that you are one fortunate gal?" she said out loud. "Here you are, ready to go downstairs in just a very few minutes, and you'll be having breakfast with the man you plan to spend the rest of your life with, someone you don't deserve and who was nearly taken from you. Just imagine that, Carla Gearhart, and never, ever give Almighty God a hard time again!''

She closed her eyes.

"Lord, I could have lost him....'' she whispered. "How could I have endured that? How could I have pulled through?''

Her voice was quavering.

"You gave Him back to me, Lord,'' she continued. "Can I ever repay you for that? I don't know how right now but I await Your leading.''

She was half expecting to feel a hand on her shoulder, as before, and though she was prepared for it this time, she still jumped when that was exactly what happened, someone placing a hand on her left shoulder, freezing her where she sat.

Enjoy him, Carla....

This time, there seemed a melancholy edge to the voice.

"I will,'' she said, pretending that she had noticed nothing different from the other occasions. "I will thank God for him every day of our lives together.''

Hold him, Carla....

She smiled, no longer scared, the voice especially soothing this time.

"Are you an angel?'' she asked outright.

But there was no answer, and that voice did not "speak'' again. An instant later, the hand lifted as well.

By reflex, she turned around, surveyed the one-thousand-square-foot bedroom, hoping she would notice a shadow leaving it, at the least, or a footprint in the plush scarlet rug.

No one.

Kyle believes in angels, she thought. *And they're in the Bible...Michael and Gabriel and others. After what has happened, I of all people shouldn't be hesitant. Instead, I should ask this one angel to come again, to stay at my side, as I will be by Kyle's side for now and, yes, yes, yes, for eternity.*

A call from downstairs interrupted her thoughts.

"Miss Carla!" her maid called up to her. "Mr. Kyle wants you."

She threw on a baby blue robe and hurried from the bedroom to the top of the circular staircase.

"Is Mr. Rivers in some difficulty?" she asked, heart pounding.

"No, Miss Gearhart, it's not that. He just wants to get up and sit outside, under some of the Spanish moss," the plump middle-aged woman told her, "but I said I couldn't do anything without your permission."

Carla thanked her, and added, "Tell him to give me fifteen minutes."

"Yes, ma'am."

She rushed back into the bedroom, hurriedly applied some makeup, picked a comfortable, casual dress with a yellow floral pattern against a light blue background, and then hurried downstairs to Kyle's room.

He was sitting up in bed, with the maid standing to one side, looking more than a little perturbed.

"Fannie here thinks I'm a stubborn man," he said, smiling.

"Pardon me, Miss Gearhart, but I know Mr. Kyle is stubborn," the maid said.

"But I couldn't get past her, physically or otherwise. She calls me stubborn but she's a lot like you. And *stubborn* just isn't the word!"

"Why is it so important for you to go outside now?" Carla asked.

"Because I am alive, and I want to go out and *see*

life...the birds, the swaying of the trees, whatever it is that's natural and alive," Kyle told her.

Fannie glanced at Carla.

"If he just weren't so good-looking," Carla said, sighing.

Kyle's wheelchair was near the other side of the bed. Carla walked over and brought it to him.

It took the two of them to lift him up and put him in it.

"Thank you, Fannie," Carla said. "I can take care of everything now."

The woman walked toward the bedroom door, then stopped.

"I pray that the good Lord will guide and protect you both," she told them. "I've seen some fine young couples in my life but none who seem as happy as the two of you when you're together."

After Fannie left, Kyle said, "She's right. We have arguments but we always end up in one another's arms afterward."

Carla pushed the wheelchair out of the bedroom and toward the back of the house. A large glass double door on one side of the kitchen faced the rear of her property.

"It's a beautiful morning," she told him as she slid it open, then slowly pushed the chair outside.

"It is, Carla," Kyle said, his mood, she thought, bordering on melancholic.

"Are you all right?" she asked.

"I have every reason to be, don't I?"

"That's not an answer," she replied as she pulled over a low-slung canvas director's chair and sat beside him.

"I guess it isn't."

"You're out of the hospital, and on the way to recovery," Carla reminded him. "What could be wrong?"

"It's hard to describe."

"Do your best."

"I should be taking care of you," Kyle told her.

"The old macho thing again?" she asked with distaste.

"It's not that at all. I love you, Carla. I have always thought of marriage as the ultimate promise on my part to take care of you."

"So, marriage is only about what the husband will do for the wife?"

"Of course not."

"Then why say what you did, why feel as you do?"

He sighed as he asked her, "Are we getting into another argument?"

"I didn't start this."

"Are you saying that I did?"

Without warning, and as a surprise to himself and to her, Kyle started sobbing. Carla held him tightly, whispering into his ear, "Let it come out. Don't hold back. We'll deal with whatever's wrong."

"I found out two days ago that my parents are getting a divorce," he moaned in obvious anguish.

"You didn't say anything. Why not tell me, Kyle? I think I could have helped you through this."

"Carla, they were married for twenty-five years! They're Christians, believing the same things I do. We go to the same spiritual well day after day. And yet—"

Now she could understood clearly, now she knew why he had been seeming so contentious.

"And you wonder if the same thing will happen to us sooner or later," she said, certain that she had caught on.

"Of course I do!" he exclaimed. "I lived with them day in and day out for more than twenty years and I never noticed anything going wrong between them. Now, suddenly, *this* happens!"

"Maybe—" Carla started to say something, then stopped herself.

"Go ahead," he asked her.

"I may be out of line."

"All right, you've warned me. Please say it."

"You might have been what held them together. You might have been the only reason they didn't split a long time ago."

He had stopped sobbing.

"And so I leave behind me the wreckage of what they once had between them? How can I face that kind of guilt, Carla?"

"And how could they have waited until now, when you are recuperating from—"

"Nearly dying?" he interrupted. "Don't blame them for that. A friend confided in me. I'm not upset that he did. He was doing the only thing he knew how, whether his timing was insensitive or not."

"I feel like I've been mean to you over the past day or so," she said.

"How could you think that?"

"We've argued."

"I was part of that. Maybe I was the mean one."

She kissed him.

"I think I wanted our relationship to be perfect," Carla remarked. "I wasn't prepared for any imperfections."

"Carla?"

"Yes?" she replied, bracing herself.

"I never wanted to seem like a weakling to you. And, yet, that's exactly what I've been for the better part of a month now."

She slipped off the director's chair and got on her knees as she held his hand.

"You had been hit by a car!" she said, annoyed and angry, but mostly just concerned. "You were probably clinically dead at one point. Your body has suffered far more than most men would be able to endure without dying, and staying that way. The Lord we both love brought you back.''

"But will I ever sing again, Carla?" he spoke sadly. "Will I ever father children with you?"

"Even if you do neither, is that really the end of everything? Is singing your whole life, Kyle? If it is, then Jesus isn't at the center of it, despite what you've been telling me all these weeks.

"Are children your only claim to manhood? I know for sure that I would want to die at first if *I* never got to sing another note, and if it turned out that I could not be a mother, but then I would look up after the anguish of knowing drove me to my knees, and I would see you by my side and know that we could get past even that."

Carla's passionate feelings were surfacing. "Am I any stronger than you? Is singing more important to you than it is to me for more than ten years?"

"Carla, please—!"

"Let me finish. I'm not heading where you think I am."

"Okay..." he said meekly.

"Kyle, Kyle, maybe I'm not strong enough to survive losing my career, maybe never having children is a blow that I couldn't take...if I had to face any of that *alone*, Kyle. You know something, though, I'm not alone, my love.

"You and I can be strong together. Isn't that a large part of what the relationship between us is going to be about? I mean, through better or worse, richer or poorer, in sickness and in health?"

Kyle's eyes were open wide as he listened, and he could not conceal the admiration he was feeling for her.

"Carla...?"

"Yes?"

"I want to hold you."

"But the doctors said we had to be very careful until your body was completely back to normal."

"I know that. I still want to hold you. Please sit on my lap."

"Will the wheelchair hold us both?"

"Have faith, Carla."

"But does having faith mean we should be careless?"

"I still want to—"

"Isn't that tempting God?" she said.

He had been leaning forward, holding his arms out. Now he fell back hard against the chair.

"You're right," he agreed reluctantly.

"Your nervous system…"

"Yes, we need to see how it goes."

"Kyle, you may not get better."

Until then, the two of them had not talked about Kyle's condition in the aftermath of what had happened at the hospital, both guilty of delaying any discussion until doing so was no longer possible. That topic was, in some respects, the serpent in the Eden that they were trying to reconstruct for them, and it could not be allowed to intrude.

"I think we both have been pretending that the immediate crisis was the only one," Kyle said, "that once we got through it, we'd be free and clear."

"I *want* to have you squeeze me so tight that I have to gasp for breath," she said wistfully, "but if we are going to beat this condition—"

"But if—" he interrupted. "Terrible words, Carla. How often do they amount to anything but hope unfulfilled, dreams torn apart and—?"

He was shaking.

"Kyle, are you cold?" Carla asked, alarmed.

"No, just thinking, just remembering what it was like only a month ago."

He held his hand out for her and, still sitting on the director's chair, she let him fold his fingers around her own.

"So recently…" he spoke in a husky tone, "but so far, far away."

"In a galaxy…" Carla started to say in an attempt at humor that she did not pursue any further, but sat there quietly with him, the two of them holding hands as tightly as they dared that morning, while remembering, cherishing….

Chapter Thirteen

Kyle graduated to walking without crutches within three and a half weeks. And he was able to discard a cane by the end of the second month after he had been released from the hospital.

"You're doing so well!" Carla exclaimed as they were playing Ping-Pong one afternoon, the game ideal exercise for him, using the muscles that he needed to build up, but without much danger of injury unless he was actually clumsy, and being *that* just was not in Kyle's makeup.

"I feel a lot better," he told her. "Why don't we go to church this Sunday? We've been away too long."

Carla wondered when he would pop that question. She had been attending church irregularly since she was a child but, later, when she was old enough to know what was going on, she found herself focusing pretty much on the blatant hypocrisies that she saw displayed around her, it seemed, week after week.

How could they do this? she thought every so often over the years. *How many people have had their faith destroyed as a result?*

"I've been putting it off," she admitted.

"Yes, I know," Kyle told her. "Prior to the accident, we went twice, period. But that was before you changed your outlook on matters of faith. Now you and I are on the same side, and I think you should go more often. I have had a physical reason *not* to go, but you could have slipped away for a couple of hours."

One of the advantages of a relationship such as the one the two of them enjoyed was the degree of candor that they had come to regard as precious but it sometimes hurt, as they were finding out.

"There is so much deceit in churches," Carla told him.

"I agree," he told her without hesitation. "I visited half a dozen until I found the right one."

"I think, during the past few years, most of those TV preachers turned me against public worship more than ever."

Kyle was silent for a moment, then he said, "I agree. They mock true worship by and large, making it seem more like a nightclub act than anything else. I think the Lord Himself stands by, watches and is ashamed."

Carla was chuckling.

"The one who claims to do all those healings. He blows on people, and they fall down. How silly! Maybe he has bad breath or something."

"I couldn't agree more. Disgusting—the lies he spews forth, the people who are duped."

"It must hurt you to say that, Kyle."

"It does, it hurts more than I can express, even to you. To get up there before millions of people and do what they do in an atmosphere more suitable for a carnival...how many people are turned off Christianity as a result? We'll never know, of course, but it has to be a lot, Carla, a whole lot."

"Kyle? I'll go this Sunday, if you feel up to it."

"Wonderful, Carla! You make me so happy."

"That's what I want to do for the rest of my life."

"And I want you to be happy. Don't ever hold back if something's bothering you, understood, my love?"

"I promise not to, whatever it is. I'll give it to you full blast."

That was how things were then but it had not been easy.

The week before, Carla ran right up against a stark short-coming of Kyle's that they would learn to deal with but before that happened, it caused at least one major league flare-up between them.

Kyle said goodbye to the middle-aged Danish female therapist he had been using, and sat back on the exercise bench that was one of several pieces of equipment Carla had bought for him as an advance wedding present. He felt awkward about accepting the range and quality of what she was having sent over but his reasoning collapsed before her obvious devotion to him. Besides, the barbells and exercise bench and all the rest would speed his recovery, and he could not argue with that.

Wow! she exclaimed to herself as she paused in the doorway of the downstairs recreation room that had been turned into a formal home gym.

Kyle had taken his shirt off and was rubbing his forehead with it.

Every muscle was pumped, with little beads of perspiration slowly dripping from his lightly hairy chest, and he was breathing heavily.

I want to rush up to you, she thought, *and hold you close and tell you that I can't stand another minute of waiting and yet—*

She could not do that to him, because, afterward, their vows would seem like meaningless words, and they both undoubtedly would face a surge of guilt that was not what they wanted to characterize their life together.

Am I more and more under Your control, Lord? Carla asked herself. *I can't believe that I'm just standing here, and not reaching for him.*

A few minutes, right after Kyle showered, the two of them were taking a walk around Carla's expansive property, looking in on her horses, feeding the birds that came by at that same time just prior to dusk, enjoying the smell of jasmine floating on a soft breeze.

Such moments proved among the finest they experienced, quiet, and loving, isolated from everyone but themselves.

But on that particular night, this serene time between them was not to last very long.

"I wonder if things will *ever* change for me," he said after they had headed back to the spa. "It's the same exercise again and again...so boring."

Carla chose to ignore it the first time he had said something like that a couple of days earlier, but this time it got to her.

"There's an alternative," she told him, gritting her teeth.

"Yeah? I'm ready. What is it?" he asked, thinking that she was going to give him a pleasant surprise.

"Being dead and buried."

"*What?*"

"You act as though this is a terrible burden."

Kyle knew that he was not handling his end of the discussion well, and tried to say, "Well, I meant—"

But Carla would not let him get any further than that.

"Whatever happened to waiting on the Lord, Kyle?" she demanded. "Have you conveniently forgotten it?"

"I'm used to activity," he tried to explain. "I feel like a prisoner. I used to get up and play basketball with some friends, or have a night out at the movies, with pizza or hot dogs, and we'd drive around until midnight or later.''

"You feel like some kind of prisoner?" she repeated. "Does that make me some kind of warden?"

"It's not that. I—"

Carla interrupted him yet again.

"This is real macho of you," she spoke with contempt. "You've pulled right out of the valley of the shadow of death, and yet you're complaining, as though the work you're doing now to recover is too much of a price to pay."

"Am I acting ungrateful?"

"That's one way to put it!"

"I'm not usually like this."

"And I can guess why."

"Tell me...."

"You're so good-looking, with such a terrific personality that you can usually have anything you want out of people and life itself, I suppose. You get an idea that you want to teach and you get job offers from five different colleges. Write a song, and it's accepted by the very first publisher you send it to.

"That's the way it's been from the beginning. In college, you were a top basketball star *and* president of the student government. There was *nothing*, Kyle, that you did not achieve if you wanted to go after it."

He was sitting in the spa, with Carla on the tiled edge, her long, still impressive legs dangling over the side.

"I was handed to you, frankly," she confessed to Kyle as he pushed his way over to her, and started kissing both her feet, which not unsurprisingly played immediate havoc with her train of thought.

"What was I saying?" she asked.

His manner was getting to her. It *always* got to her.

Good thing we pledged to save sex until marriage, she

thought. *We could have given the neighbors a whole lot to gossip about!*

Carla pulled away from him because she did not want to be distracted.

"I am trying to be *very* serious here," she said.

"How can you expect *me* to act the same way with your legs looking as they do? And the rest of you even more gorgeous?"

"You'll have to *try* to listen." She sighed. "I don't think you deliberately manipulate people. Maybe this happens unconsciously. Which is exactly why you're doing that right now, I mean, trying to get my mind off what we were discussing, because it's a subject that makes you a little uncomfortable. But I have to tell you the truth, Kyle. Sometimes you act like a spoiled brat."

No one had ever talked to him like that. He had been the golden boy at every stage of his life for so long that he seemed insulated from such criticism. The miracle was that he had not become insufferably arrogant, something that could be credited to the semblance of humility his faith imposed upon him.

"Just because I'm bored with all this rehab stuff?" he answered feebly.

"You said it, I didn't."

"And that means I'm being ungrateful to the Lord?"

Whatever anyone did say to him in mild rebuke over the years, none of it was aimed at any aspect of his religious convictions. And yet that was essentially what Carla was doing, making him uncomfortable.

"I think it does," she told him.

He could have argued with her, just for the sake of not giving in too quickly, but he avoided doing this because there was more than an edge of truth in what Carla was telling him, and he needed to listen to her.

"I suppose you might be right," Kyle acknowledged freely. "How obnoxious have I been?"

Carla winced at his use of the word *obnoxious* for he had never been that, as far as she was concerned.

"It's just stuff I've noticed," she said. "Stuff that, you know, other people have never spotted in you. But then I'm more involved with you than anyone except your parents have been, I guess."

"You think they've not been honest with me all this time," Kyle spoke, genuinely disturbed.

"It's part of life, you know. You're invited to a party, and when you arrive, you're introduced to the host. You need to say something, and so you tell her, 'What a lovely dress you're wearing.' It may be a perfectly frumpy thing, incorporating a bad choice of colors, but you say that anyway."

He pulled himself up on the edge of the spa, looking so depressed that Carla began to wonder about the wisdom of confronting him.

Do I have any right to talk to him like this? she asked herself. *I never suspected that he would bruise so easily.*

"Gosh, Carla..." Kyle started to speak.

"Forgive me," she asked.

"I'm looking at myself in a mirror, and all I can see are the blemishes."

Something seemed to have gone out of him as he talked.

"There is so much that is wonderful about you," she said.

"But a lot that isn't."

"You aren't expecting yourself to be perfect, are you?"

"Of course not! I just didn't think I was as flawed as I'm seeing is the case now."

He was shivering.

"I wanted to be everything I could for you," he said somberly.

"You *are,* my love," Carla assured him, panicking a bit.

"I'm going back inside now," he said in a monotone.

As he stood, and walked toward the sliding glass door that led into the house, he turned for a moment, and looked sadly at her, and then was gone from sight.

Carla wanted to rush after him, wanted to hold him in her arms and apologize but then while her manner might have been improved upon, what she had told him was true. He was taking it the wrong way but that was Kyle's responsibility, not hers.

She wondered if she should go after him right away but decided that waiting a bit was probably the better idea.

Oh, Lord, please heal us, she prayed. *Please step in and don't let this go any further. I need Kyle, and I think he needs me. Please help us. We are just trying to be honest with one another but I think I hurt him, I hurt him badly. Show me more wisdom, and touch his emotions with your sweet touch, Lord.*

She had changed into some casual clothes and was sitting in the family room, with its wall-to-wall aged brick fireplace and hardwood floor, trying to deal with her emotions when Kyle appeared in the doorway, and said, "Hi."

She looked up from the leather-surfaced couch on which she was sitting, and smiled as she replied, "Hi, good-looking."

"I'm sorry," he said as he walked toward her.

"No, Kyle, I'm the one who needs to say that," she told him. "I've been trying to deal with some things that most people take years to sort out. I guess I didn't want married life to be anything less than ideal, and so I tried to clean out everything *before* we became husband and wife."

Dressed in shorts and a tank top, he sat down next to her.

"I'm glad you did," he said. "I was just spending some time with the Lord, and asking Him to do with me as He would, open up my heart when it's been closed, and I think now, Carla, that you're mostly right with what you said an hour ago. People seem happier making me this remarkable, ideal creation, with few flaws, because it satisfies them.''

"Kyle..."

"Yes, dear, dear Carla?"

"The more perfect you are, the better *they* are going to feel. It's nothing deliberate. I mean, you *are* very special, and so they don't have to work too hard at that."

"When did you put all *that* together?" he asked, smiling broadly.

"Pretty confused?"

"Well, yes, a little but I think the truth's in there somewhere."

Both started laughing heartily.

"Start me going, and it's hard to stop me."

"Well, I certainly hope so," he said.

She had lost count of how many times he had gotten her to blush, and now another had to be added to the list.

"You're a bit of a scoundrel!" she chided him.

"Me?"

"A touch of one maybe."

It felt good for them to be in the kind of mood that was now showing itself between them.

"Kyle, my love, you have no exclusive claim to all the faults that may exist in our relationship, and if you ever want to discuss mine, that's fine with me," she said. "I mean, *are* you okay with this?"

"We're going to be so happy together," he remarked, "and I think we will be in love fifty years from now as much as we are today, as we sit back and hear the sounds of our children all over the house."

They did nothing more then than hold one another, no words spoken, flames from the fireplace casting dancing images over their bodies, the muted ticking of an antique grandfather clock the only sound apart from an occasional spitting as tree sap ignited briefly, until they fell asleep together, to be awakened hours later only by the insistent sound of a rooster from a nearby farm as dawn spread its early light over the land.

Chapter Fourteen

After seeing their earlier plans wrecked by Kyle's accident, Carla and he decided to set a new date for the wedding, exactly three months after he was released from the
hospital. Kyle planned to ask the Reverend David Fetherston, a tall, thin, square-jawed Englishman who had lived
in the United States more than half his life, to officiate.
They attended the Sunday service and had made plans to
meet the reverend afterward.

Carla had enjoyed the service, highlighted by its concen-
tration on the joy of faith which was imparted by hymns
and other melodies as well as testimonies of praise and
thanksgiving, with a sermon that empathized personal integrity as one of the greatest gifts anyone could give to
God. When the service ended she was eager to meet with
the minister.

Since Carla had no able parents, and Kyle's mother and
father were missionaries serving in the Far East, they had
to discuss the matter of paying for the ceremony and the
reception afterward.

"Wait for me back in my study," the Reverend Fetherston told them after the Sunday service. "I am sure we can work out the details."

Carla could have paid for five weddings and a funeral out of one of her petty cash accounts. But she hesitated to suggest this to Kyle since it really would open up a can of worms. He was already sensitive about making her home, a mansion by any reasonable guideline, his own, and probably never being able to provide for her in any way equal to the standard that she had known for years.

It seemed an insoluble dilemma, until the Reverend Fetherston had a suggestion that should have seemed obvious.

"Elope," he said simply. "I did. As a struggling young seminary student, I didn't have the money for a full-scale wedding."

Kyle nodded appreciatively, and then said, "Carla could pay for it easily but I don't think that's proper. A man should—"

"—be able to provide for everything," the pastor interrupted. "Isn't that what you were going to say?"

"Something like that, sir."

"What about sharing things?"

"How do you mean that, sir?"

"Why not share the expenses?"

"But I have very little money."

The Reverend Fetherston leaned back in his chair.

"So getting married to Carla isn't an economic thing for you, is that right? You're not marrying her for her money, and yet that money will always be right. You're going to live in a million-dollar house, and your wife is going to dress in gowns and other clothes worth tens of thousands of dollars. As I understand it, she owns a Bentley, a Jaguar and other cars. Yet none of this has stopped you from making plans to be married."

"You're right, sir."

"Then why let a wedding *become* an economic thing, a stumbling block if all the rest is not?"

"But you suggested eloping."

"I did, but my circumstances were entirely different from yours. Carla isn't the eloping kind, Kyle. She wants a wedding in a church, and all the trimmings. Don't deny her that. It could backfire years from now, son."

"I just don't have the money, sir."

"Kyle, you're a proud man, and I understand that. Let Carla provide a few ingredients, and you do what you can."

It was apparent that Kyle still resisted that notion. But the pastor was not willing to admit defeat.

"Kyle, Kyle, you *are* a man of great faith, but you mustn't let your pride do you in. A marriage involves each partner bringing to the union whatever they can. How many wives have helped to support their husbands while they went to medical school, for example. Were those men emasculated as a result?

"Of course not, son. It is, in such cases, something done out of love. Let Carla show you that love any way she can. Don't you want the same privilege? To demonstrate how much you love her by doing some insane and extravagant act that arises from your passion, not your ego or even your common sense?"

The pastor was smiling.

"If you're still uncertain, let me say something that the Lord has just put in my heart, okay?"

"Go ahead, sir."

"If her parents were able, they'd be financing everything, am I correct?"

Kyle nodded solemnly.

"Then don't punish Carla because of the fact that they are sick and are no longer able to plan the type of wedding their daughter would have asked for. Am I making sense?"

"Yes, sir, you are."

"I think you ought to do whatever your parents would have done if they were able. I am sure they would be very pleased."

He returned his attention to Kyle.

"Is this satisfactory with you, young man?" he asked pleasantly.

"How could I object?" Kyle responded. "Praise God for your wisdom!"

The pastor did not accept any responsibility.

"We are urged to have the mind of God as much as our sinful nature will allow us," he said. "If I have helped, then I am glad but I was simply empowered by God."

The Reverend Fetherston asked that they close in prayer. He started out, and then Kyle prayed out loud. Finally it was Carla's turn.

"Lord, we *are* grateful to You for Your provision for us," she nearly whispered. "We know that You are aware of everything, from the beginning to the end and all that happens between those times. May Your Will be done in our lives, and may we acknowledge You to others whenever we have the opportunity."

When Carla had finished, she opened her eyes, and saw Kyle and the Reverend Fetherston smiling.

"Did I say something funny?" she asked apprehensively.

"We're not smiling because you amused us," Kyle told her, "but because our spirits were touched, and invigorated."

"No one has ever said that about me before."

"But it *is* true, Carla, and as you grow in the Lord, it will become more and more so, my love."

After saying goodbye to the pastor, Carla and Kyle headed for her car which was in the church parking lot.

"It's all so changed," she said as they got inside.

"In what way?" asked Kyle.

"A church like that, a man like you by my side, the hope of marriage, which I thought would never happen to me—but if it did, it couldn't possibly last, and would become one of those dreary show biz statistics—these are real, and they make me feel good. I also feel clean, Kyle, I mean, really clean."

A church like that, a man like you by my side, the hope of marriage soon, which I thought would never happen to me—but if it did, it couldn't possibly last, and would become another dreary show biz statistics—these are real, and they make me feel good. I also feel clean, Kyle, I mean, really clean.

Later, at night, Carla was in her bedroom, not able to sleep, and so she got up, went over to a bureau dresser, and opened one of the drawers.

Scrapbooks.

Several of these. Each one was filled with clips about her career, from the earliest days to the present, especially the reviews she got for one arena performance or another and, of course, the coverage she was accorded after winning an Oscar.

Years of memories...

Carla remembered the first one-night engagements that resourceful Irving Chicolte had been able to book for her, mediocre gigs when she would be only a backup for one of the singers or groups, going onstage when they were ill or delayed by air traffic or weather, but otherwise having to content herself with waiting for the next chance to show paying customers what she could do.

When she finally entered the spotlight on such sporadic occasions, she generally wore a silver-sequined dress that was eye-catching enough by itself but when combined with her brilliant long red hair made Carla an unrelentingly spellbinding figure on stage, silencing all conversation as au-

audiences were first drawn by her look and then held by her voice, which seemed as much operatic in its power as it was country.

Chattanooga, New Orleans, Dallas...the cities became a dizzying cavalcade of airports, bus stops, rented automobiles...whatever means of transportation could get her from one location to another, only to stand backstage and never get to sing a note. She was paid for being available and so she was not starving at any point during the first year or so, the only havoc she experienced hitting her emotions instead, a long, wearying period of paying her dues that tested her stamina as well as her determination.

And look how different life is for me now, she thought.

All around her were the trappings of her multimillion-dollar-a-year status: furniture that was handmade; the finest grade of carpeting; wood paneling as well as special wallpaper with a country music theme; a full household staff; a movie screening theater; all her cars; and much more.

And I will soon have a husband I shall adore for the rest of my life, she told herself happily.

She was about halfway through the first scrapbook when she heard the voice again, as unexpectedly as before.

Soon these will no longer matter, Carla....

Just as startled this time, as in the other instances, she waited for the touch of a hand, and wasn't disappointed.

"What do you mean?" she asked expectantly. "That Kyle and I will be building a new life for ourselves?"

So much of what you are is built upon press clippings and applauding audiences, Carla....

Her hands were becoming wet, and she carefully put that one album back in the drawer with the others.

"I've lived for my reviews in the morning after a performance," she acknowledged. "A good review made my day perfect, a bad one destroyed it."

So foolish...

"Yes, yes, I know that, but I've never known anything else," Carla hastened to add. "I started performing when I was just a teenager on "New Star," that series on television. And I won. Since then, it has been a question of trying to win, win, win all the time. The Oscar was my ultimate vindication."

And there is nothing left for you, Carla?

She shivered as the voice spoke those words.

"I thought that that might be the case until I met Kyle," she said. "He's changed everything."

Is he just another trophy or plaque for you?

She reacted angrily, saying, "That's nonsense! I love Kyle."

Do you love him, Carla? Or do you just love the idea of being loved by someone as young and vital as he is?

She slammed a fist down on top of the bureau.

"Who are you?" she demanded. "You come into my life whenever you wish, and insinuate what I know is nothing more than claptrap."

The hand left her shoulder. And the voice did not speak again that evening.

As Carla stood beside the dresser, she was shivering.

Chapter Fifteen

Finally, Carla and Kyle found themselves with the luxury of thinking about little but their wedding.

She had had two previous marriages, so it was not a new experience for her. And she was a much sought after guest at any number of Nashville and Hollywood high-profile weddings involving major music and movie people.

Kyle was the problem.

A nervous wreck...

He went through mood swings ranging from wildly exuberant to something approaching depression. She had not seen the latter before but knowing that he had this dark side made him seen rather more human, not a perfect example of a perfect man.

"What if something else happens?" he would moan. "What if the testing we've had so far is not over?"

So many "what ifs" that Carla was tempted to take over altogether but then they had already faced that tendency of hers to be a control freak and she was not about to risk it again. So she chose to overlook Kyle's prewedding jitters.

Any such vulnerability Kyle showed made him all the more appealing to her.

"You are wonderful," she told him more than once when he was in the middle of one of his moods.

"Even when I'm acting like a fool?" he asked.

"You're *my* fool."

A week before the wedding, Roxie Chicolte flew in from Beverly Hills to lend her help to the planning. She had been the brains behind some of the biggest events in the entertainment industry, including other notable celebrity weddings.

Roxie also had had a hand in the Academy Awards presentations for a number of years, working with the most famous producer in the business.

"It's a great opportunity," she said, laughing. "Look at all those potential clients under one roof, many of them seething with dissatisfaction at their present agents. I look, I listen, then I move in, opening them for Irving to come along."

Roxie was able to spend as much time with Kyle as with Carla, getting to know him well enough.

"I can see why Carla adores you," she said as they stood in the midst of a rose garden that he had started while he was convalescing at the house. "I don't doubt for a New York minute your masculinity but then you have this sweet side."

"Sweet?" he asked. "Am I so sweet?"

"Oh, yes, you are. The way you putter around these rosebushes and trees. You actually care about them."

"I do. They are among God's gifts to the world. They show His handiwork in every petal, the way these fit together so perfectly that could not have come about by coincidence or accident. Nothing like that *evolves*, Roxie, it is *designed*."

"But there is so much pain in this world," Roxie observed. "Was that part of the perfect design, too?"

Kyle just then pricked his finger on a thorn.

"Not bad timing," he chuckled, not meaning to trivialize what she had said.

"So you hurt your finger, so what? If that's the worst you ever—"

Roxie cut herself off and then added, "I'm sorry about that. You've been closer to death than most people. I had no right to say—"

"Relax," he interrupted her. "Nothing you say could ever upset me. We are bonded, you and Irving and Carla and I. That will be the case so long as you and I live."

"Sounds like marriage!"

"In some respects it is. Friendship, after all, is a more important part of marriage than sex."

"Well, I don't know about that!" she exclaimed.

"By the way, that pain I just felt..."

"Yes, Kyle?"

"If I didn't hurt when I pricked my finger, and I am now warned to be more careful as a result, what would happen?"

"You might prick yourself again."

"And again, right?"

"I suppose, but I don't see what you're getting at."

"So what does all this tell us? That pain is God's way of alerting us to something wrong with our body. If there were no pain, we would die of conditions and such that tell us we need to get medical attention pronto."

Roxie and he sat down on two folding chairs in the midst of that new rose garden. Most of the plants had been bought already in bloom, and their scents were mingling in the air, like a natural perfume.

"So lovely..." Roxie remarked.

"I think that's how it will be in heaven," Kyle told her.

"We will approach the pearly gates, stand for a moment, and sniff the sweet, pure air."

"If only..."

"If only you could believe, Roxie?"

She no longer was surprised at how intuitive this man was. Every so often she caught a glimpse of why Carla had found him so charming.

"Something like that," she admitted.

"I think you will in time."

"Me?" For the first time, she thought he might be saying something out of rote, not honest feelings. "Oh, yes, you. I have a good feeling about your eternal destiny."

"You can't be serious."

"I am *very* serious."

Whatever his sincerity, or lack of it, Roxie found him bordering arrogance.

"I will never believe!" she declared. "I know too much about real life ever to believe a fantasy."

"Don't box yourself in."

"Reality all around me argues against—" she started to say, then looked at him, and stopped once again, a touch of shame gripping her.

"Sorry," she said. "You have every right to believe as you do. And I have every right not to accept any of it."

"Free will," Kyle agreed. "Greatest argument for the existence of a loving, forgiving, grace-filled Creator."

"To believe, I will have to experience something so compelling that it would be idiotic for me to turn away."

"You want faith without having the need for faith."

"Does that make sense, Kyle?"

"To put it another way, you want proof so that blind faith is no longer necessary. Well, I don't think God rules that out frankly, although it surely isn't His preference. In the New Testament, an apostle named Thomas needed to have proof that—"

For the time being, Roxie had had enough.

"It's getting a little chilly," she interrupted, "I'm going inside now."

"Sorry..." he told her.

"We won't decide what people have debated for centuries."

"Roxie?"

"Yes, Kyle?"

"I decided years ago. You're the one who's uncertain."

"You can't know that. Besides, it's not true."

"I *do* know, and, yes, it *is* true. Your mind refuses to tolerate what your heart already knows."

"Because of what you went through, your miraculous recovery?"

"I would not have put it that way but, yes, I'd agree with that."

Roxie seemed ready to say something else but turned away and went back inside the house.

Kyle thought he detected the hint of tears in her eyes.

As it turned out, Carla's and Kyle's originally planned site for their wedding, the church building where he regularly attended services, was far too small for what proved to be the final guest list. The people Carla wanted to invite numbered into the hundreds; those Roxie and Irving Chicolte hoped to have brought the total to near a thousand. And, still, Kyle's own group had to be counted.

"What do we do?" Roxie asked Carla as they both sat on a comfortable sofa.

"We have to change the location."

"But that means we need to let people know."

"Of course."

"They're coming in from all over the world, Carla."

"I know that."

"But we have to tell them what's going on."

"Then hire a temp service. Better yet, hire an *entire* temp service. Have everyone working with them involved. And offer them a bonus!"

"That could be very expensive."

"So, at $35 million-plus a year in income, I can't afford it. Is that what you're telling me?"

"No way, Carla. But it's going to be touch-and-go. Some people may already have left, you know."

"For next week?"

"If they're flying in from Switzerland and other countries, that's possible, because they may be scheduling stops along the way."

"We'll do it, Carla. If we need fifty temps, we'll get them."

Roxie leaned back against the back of the sofa, and stared at her.

"What's wrong?" Carla asked self-consciously.

"You *are* amazing! I've not seen you this energized since you won the Oscar."

"Roxie, Kyle is my love. I adore him. I want this to be perfect."

"Doesn't he rankle under the kind of control that you're having?"

"A little, but then I was reminded that the bride's family generally planned everything anyway."

"Am I suddenly your secret mother?"

"I guess so. You've been like a mother to me. Hey, why don't we just make it official. Okay?"

"Fine with me."

Later that day, they decided on the new site: a small arena that had been built on the outskirts of Nashville, essentially Grand Ole Opry-like, with a bit less than one thousand seats arranged amphitheater-style around a stage in the middle.

"I'm nervous," Carla admitted.

"Why?" Roxie asked. "It's being handed to us for nothing except the cost of ushers and other employees. What's not to like? The owners adore you. They don't want to make a profit from your wedding."

"It's not me. Kyle might not."

"Why?"

"Too show businessy. It plays right into the hands of the tabloids."

Roxie paused, thinking about what Carla just told her.

"Do you want to suggest it to him? Or should I?"

"I'll do it, Roxie. I think, though, that we should line up alternatives."

"A week before the wedding?"

"What else can we do?"

"Test whether Kyle wants you to be happy more than he needs to cling to his foibles. Is that plain enough?"

Carla nodded, appreciating her friend's honesty but dreading how Kyle would respond.

She need not have been concerned.

When Kyle heard what was in her heart, and how much turmoil she had created for herself by worrying about his own feelings, he told her that he could not possibly love her more than he did at that very moment.

"Nothing can stand in our way now," he said. "I am feeling real good. Everything I think about these days has you at the center, and the Lord over both of us."

…you at the center.

None of her other men had ever made Carla feel as Kyle did. Some of them might have made him look naive and unsophisticated but that was if she looked only at outward appearances. When she judged the inner man he proved most of the others downright selfish and, in their way, far more immature and shallow.

In a few hours less than a week, the two of them would become husband and wife at the Nashville Music Arena.

Afterward, they planned to honeymoon in Hawaii on the island of Maui.

Suddenly, a week did seem like an eternity....

Chapter Sixteen

Eleven hundred and twenty-five people attended the wedding of Carla Gearhart and Kyle Rivers. An army of parking attendants took care of the crush of luxury cars of every make and description. Security guards and undercover bomb squad members from the Nashville Police Department were plentiful because a threat about a hidden explosive device was received and taken very seriously but, soon enough, proven to be a hoax.

Media coverage was extraordinary.

"Entertainment Tonight," "Access Hollywood," "Inside TV" and a dozen other programs from the United States and around the world were present. The wire services, the supermarket tabloids, such publications as *Entertainment Weekly, US, People* and others all had sent reporters and photographers.

The list of guests was, of course, the magnet, and was definitely a list that encompassed many of the top stars, including some fellow Academy Award, Emmy and Tony award winners, in addition to Carla herself.

As the guests entered and found their seats, a famous

pianist, a close friend to both Carla and Kyle played a composition of his that seemed like an instrumental combination of "Amazing Grace" and "How Great Thou Art," the rendition so beautiful that scores of guests were conspicuously dabbing their eyes with handkerchiefs while he was at the Steinway.

And, then, finally, Carla Gearhart and Kyle Rivers pledged their vows as husband and wife....

Virtually everyone had seen Carla any number of times in person.

However, few had met Kyle before that night. And the scuttlebutt during the hours afterward indicated that he had more impact than any of the high-powered stars who were attending.

"Who *is* that guy?" an associate of a top-rated star gasped. "He is the most gorgeous man I have ever seen!"

Others responded in a similar manner, bemoaning the fact that Carla had gotten to him before *they* ever had a chance.

At the reception, not less than five producers passed Kyle handwritten notes, asking him if he was available to come to Hollywood. He was unprepared for anything like that. After all, it was a wedding, not an audition. Irving Chicolte put a stop to what was happening by politely telling the other agents that all inquiries were to go through him.

Uncharacteristically, he apologized later directly to Kyle for not getting permission beforehand.

"That's fine," Kyle told him. "I don't think any of us expected this sort of thing. You probably saved me from having to deal with a bunch of others before it was all over. I'm thankful, Irving, not upset."

"It was still wrong on my part," Irving said with a contrition that was not part of any act. "It won't happen again."

"Irving?"

"Yes, my friend?"

"I would trust you with my life."

For a moment Irving could not open his mouth, could not say anything, then finally, he told Kyle, "You have no idea how foolish that would sound to so many people where I come from."

"I don't care about *their* reactions. I just know the kind of man *you* really are. Tell me, have you ever once cheated Carla?"

"Never!"

"Then I doubt that you will start with me."

"How interested *would* you be in an acting career?"

"Exciting idea. Maybe Carla and I could do a movie together."

Irving blinked. "Seriously?"

Kyle laughed and slapped Irving on the arm. "Only kidding, Irving. Acting's not my style. More than one Oscar on the mantel looks a little tacky, don't you think?" he teased.

It was time for Carla and Kyle Rivers to leave for the airport.

Irving had purchased the tickets the previous week, and was reaching into the inside pocket of his tuxedo for them.

"What airline?" she asked.

"I have something of a surprise for you, my dear," Irving told her.

"What in the world have you done?" Carla asked expectantly.

"I hired a former MGM Grand plane, and the pilot and crew are making a special trip for you. It's my treat, dear."

"The whole plane all to ourselves?"

"Exactly. No fans to bother you. The best food in the air. And no delays getting off the ground here in Nashville."

"Irving?"

"Yes?"

"I love you!"

Carla hugged him as the longtime and cherished friend he was but this time with even more caring.

"Be happy," he whispered. "You deserve each other. You're both wonderful, wonderful people."

"You sound like Lawrence Welk!"

"I think he would have loved you, Carla. And he would have adored Kyle. He was very big on vital young people."

Roxie walked up to them.

"It's a struggle getting your husband away from other women," she said. "They're hanging around him three deep, I'm afraid. You've got to be on guard."

"I know that. He's special. Someone like him is bound to attract women. Look at what he did to me."

"I'm going to be like your guardian angel," Roxie told her. "Anybody who causes you pain will suffer—"

"Shush!" Carla gently admonished. "Vengeance is the Lord's."

Roxie's expression was rather odd then.

"Anything wrong?" Carla asked.

"Have you ever felt like someone has placed their hand on your shoulder, and you hear them talking almost in a whisper but when you turn around, you can't find anybody?"

"Yes, I have. Tell me about it."

"Later," Roxie told her. "I'll call you in a few days. Go now."

She kissed Carla on the cheek.

"My love and my prayers go with you," she said.

"Prayers? Are you talking to God now?"

"Trying to, dear, trying to."

Kyle joined them.

"Limo's outside," he said.

Flanked by Roxie and Irving, they managed to get through the throng. As Carla reached the sidewalk, she threw her bridal bouquet over her shoulder, and then she and Kyle climbed into the back seat of the limo.

He leaned over to kiss her.

"That's only the beginning," he said. "I wonder about, well, now, before we reach the airport."

"Are you kidding?" she asked with mock distaste. "You've got me disciplined in this waiting business. I was even thinking of suggesting that we wait until after the honeymoon."

They both broke out laughing, alive with the joy that was flooding every part of their bodies.

On the flight to Maui, Carla could not stop herself from looking at Kyle, furtively most of the time, for she was afraid that, if she avoided doing this, he might disappear from sight, or perhaps she would awaken from what had been some colossal dream, the most beguiling of her life, to find that *everything* had been little more than her hidden desires, with no reality to support them.

He is making me act like some kid, she told herself. I am a grown woman. How can he be doing this to me?

The crew continually pampered them with food that seemed fit for a banquet, including lobster and prime rib and an array of desserts that neither could resist.

"We're going to get fat," Carla groaned just before stuffing her mouth with some Dobosh torte that was the best she had had since her stay at the Sacher Hotel in Vienna, Austria, a number of years ago.

She complimented the chef—yes, a top-notch chef on the plane—and he told her that he had gotten the recipe from a friend of his who was also a chef, someone even more highly rated than he was.

"It's as good as I had in Vienna," she told him.

"I am very glad," the rotund chap named Adolfo replied. "My friend is the head chef at the Sacher Hotel."

"The Sacher—!" Carla said, thoroughly amazed at what initially seemed quite a striking coincidence, and then she realized who was behind this, adding, "Did Irving Chicolte help you arrange this?"

Adolfo smiled, and sheepishly replied, chuckling a bit, "He told us everything, Mrs. Rivers!"

"You have re-created the pastry brilliantly."

She closed her eyes for a moment.

"Actually it is so good, Adolfo, that it helps me imagine that I am back at that wonderful hotel."

This man lived for praise, and Carla's remark was what he wanted to hear.

"Thank you very much," he told her. "I am very happy that someone such as yourself who could order anything she wanted to eat from anywhere in the world is pleased with what I have done."

He paused, and then asked, "Mrs. Rivers?"

"Yes, Adolfo."

"I think you and Mr. Rivers are really very special people. You both deserve much happiness."

After Adolfo went back to the small kitchen area on the bottom level of the plane, she turned to Kyle.

"Be forewarned, my love—the Austrians did not believe one whit in sacrificing taste to reduce calories," she told him while licking her fingers of the chocolate frosting that had been spread over the torte.

"I think we'll be able to work off the calories over the next few days, trust me," he said, blushing slightly.

They kissed often during the four hours and ten minutes that they spent twenty-thousand feet above the Pacific Ocean, feeling few restrictions since the crew of the plane knowingly avoided much contact with them except for serving food and beverages.

Carla closed her eyes, thinking back over the wedding, how much of a production it seemed, that being the part she regretted, knowing as she did Kyle's sensitivities. But once she got past that, as she hoped he did before long—from the early stage with the John Tesh testimony to just before she and Kyle exchanged their vows—the sense of growing spirituality was extraordinary. It seemed to envelop the entire arena, hundreds of people caught up in it, as though a mass reformation were taking place; sour expressions being replaced by smiles, often rather serene ones.

The minister asked that anyone who had a testimony to share to stand up and give it. One after the other, more than a famous people together with largely unknown ones did just that, as though they were instead at a Billy Graham crusade. Carla herself had to get used to this part of it but once she did, she found herself with tears streaming down her cheeks while men and women told movingly of God's cleansing, redemptive power in their lives, freeing them from all kinds of burdens and addictions that had chained them for years and come close to destroying their lives.

"I can tell you that the Lord is real," announced one of the stars of a prime-time television series. "I can tell you that nothing the world has to offer compares with what He can do in someone's life if they let Him."

Then it was time for Carla and Kyle to stand before the minister and exchange their vows.

At the very beginning, seconds into the ceremony, she was overcome by her emotions and started crying.

"Are you all right?" both Kyle and the minister asked at the same time since they had no idea what was happening.

Carla nodded, then turned to face as many of the wedding guests as she could, given the circular layout of the arena.

"I know this isn't part of the script," she said, her cheeks glistening, "but I can't help it. I have to tell you how this man makes me feel. I am a new woman, a new human being because of him."

Carla cleared her throat and smiled.

"Does this mean I am depending upon him for my happiness?" she continued. "A *modern* woman doing that! Is this a throwback to a time when women weren't as liberated as they are now?

"I don't know about any of this. What I do know is that Kyle and I depend *upon one another!* He didn't need to change very much but I sure did. My awards, my platinum records, reviews of my performances were the nucleus of my life until I met him. Now it is all different. We fill one another's lives. And we have Someone with us at all times, the Lord we have come to know and love."

And then the rest of the ceremony continued as planned. When Kyle lifted Carla's veil to kiss the new bride, he wiped away the tears that were glistening on her cheeks.

"I love you with all my heart," he told her. "That will never change, for time and eternity."

The honeymoon suite at the hotel in Lahaina included a water mattress set in a bamboo frame.

After opening the door, which had a palm tree design on it, and carrying Carla inside, Kyle looked at the bed, then away.

"You aren't embarrassed, are you?" she asked, kidding him.

"No, of course not!" he exclaimed.

"But you *are!*"

And then, realizing what had made him react as he did, she said, "You've never slept on a water bed, have you?"

"No..."

"It's quite an experience."

"I'll bet."

After unpacking, they separated their clothes for storage in the walk-in his-and-hers closets.

Even Carla, a veteran of hotels all over the world, was impressed by the accommodations, especially the extravagantly oversize bathroom, with dual sinks, each of which was shaped like a giant oyster shell, and a shower that was made of lava rock, as well as the gold fixtures.

"Want to have room service send up champagne?" she asked.

"Do you think we actually need it?" he said as he brushed his teeth while Carla did the same. "I feel light-headed just looking at you."

She placed two fingers on his lips.

"I feel the same," she assured him. "Every muscle in my body is aching for you, Kyle, every nerve is crying out to feel you close right now," she said, her eyes half-closed.

"So be it!" he said suddenly, put his arms around her, lifted her up and carried her to the bed.

Afterwards, as Carla rested her head on Kyle's chest, she was not sleepy at all, neither was he, and they talked briefly until—

"Why are we chattering away like this?" he asked with mock consternation. "Plenty of time for that."

"Come to think of it, I have no idea!"

Then both started giggling.

"Talking isn't at all what I have in mind for the next few hours, my dearest," Kyle told her.

"Really?" Carla replied with surprise that was entirely feigned. "What else do you want to—?"

She did not get a chance to finish that sentence.

Chapter Seventeen

Carla had been with other men in and out of marriage, a facet of her life that she knew was forgiven but which she had not as yet been able to forget. Yet in Kyle's arms, she felt as if she were discovering love's mysteries for the first time—and learning what real love was all about. She was glad that they had waited.

And there was something else, what he had told her after they had made love for the second time.

"You know what's wonderful about tonight?" he asked.

"Well, yes, I have a pretty good idea," Carla replied with some teasing sarcasm.

He held her tightly.

"God meant for His human creations to be happy as you and I are now, for the reasons we feel as we do."

"No guilt?"

"That's right. I feel so liberated, it's...it's like nothing I've ever known before. Only redemption meant more to me. I felt ecstasy when that happened, and that's how I do feel right now."

"But my conscience used to be so hardened that I never knew much guilt anyway," Carla admitted.

"That's what plenty of people would say, my love, but I honestly feel that there could have been moments when your guard was down, and a still small voice was telling you, 'Something's wrong, something's wrong.'"

It was true. She *had* felt that way so many times, but always in the end chose to ignore that voice. She was sorry, but the past could not be changed. She could only do better in the future.

Carla opened her eyes slowly.

Something was moving at the end of the large waterbed, and it was not Kyle.

First one eye, then another.

Looking at her...

Studying every movement.

Her body tensed.

At first Carla thought it was a big rat, and she was prepared to yell for Kyle who was in the bathroom taking a shower.

The creature was sitting up on its back feet, looking then more like a thin, narrow squirrel than a rat.

Its nose was wiggling.

"Kyle!" she said, finally raising her voice but not screaming.

No answer.

"Kyle!"

Still nothing.

Her heart was beating faster.

"Ky—!"

He opened the bathroom door and she could see that he was drying himself.

"What's...that?" she asked, her voice trembling.

"A mongoose," he told her casually.

"Oh...is that supposed to make me feel better?"

"They were brought in many, many years ago to rid the islands of snakes. You can find plenty of mongooses but no snakes unless you go to the zoo."

He started to close the door, then stuck his head out.

"By the way, they're really quite harmless. They can bite, for sure, but are likely to do that only if you seem to be attacking them."

Kyle gave her a look that would have relaxed her under *any* circumstances.

"You should be pleased," he added cheerfully. "They generally are real skittish around strangers."

In a second or two, the mongoose came closer, up to her waist, and seemed ready to hop onto her shoulder.

Carla was becoming charmed by it.

"You're so brave, and curious," she said, her tone soft. "I remember, when I was a kid, that I used to bring wounded animals to Momma for help. I ended up caring for most of them myself. I was good at that!"

The mongoose seemed to be studying her.

"What is it?" Carla asked.

She noticed one of the animal's feet.

Wounded. And bleeding.

"How did you know to come to me?" she wondered.

She reached out slowly, trying to touch its body without seeming threatening. Then it shook itself mightily, and scampered off the bed and onto the floor. Carla sat on the edge of the bed, not prepared to give up.

"I'm so sorry...." she said.

It looked at her again curiously but just could not bring itself to trust her enough to let her help, so it scampered past the partially open balcony door.

Wondering how the creature, which was less by a foot in length, not including its tail, ever got up to the third floor of the hotel, Carla started to pull her nightgown more neatly around her, intending to go outside and look, then realized she was not wearing anything.

"It's been awhile," she said out loud.

She walked over to the closet and picked out a pure white cotton robe and started back toward the balcony.

The air was cool but not chilly against her face.

The mongoose was gone by the time she reached the balcony. As she glanced over the edge, she saw it hurrying across the thick green grass.

"How did you—?" she spoke before seeing the bamboo tree planted to one side of the balcony. "I'll bet that was it."

Sighing with regret that she had been unable to indulge her propensity for helping injured creatures, she walked back into the room.

"Kyle?" Carla called out. "I'm pretty hungry. Want me to call room service or should we take advantage of that delectable buffet the clerk told us about yesterday when we were checking in?"

There was no answer.

"Kyle?" she repeated.

Next, she knocked on the bathroom door, and called for him again.

No response.

Please, no, God, Carla begged. Not now, not tonight!

Suddenly—

A sound.

Moaning.

Kyle was moaning.

She swung open the door.

Kyle was on the black marble floor, his chest covered with blood.

"I...fell..." he said, looking up at her. "Hit...my... head...but...didn't...knock...myself...out. I...I...tried...

to...stand...but...my...legs...felt...all...rubbery."

Carla knelt beside him, barely able to talk but managing to say, "I'll get an ambulance right away!"

"I...love...you...." Kyle told her. "Sorry...about... all...this."

He tried to kiss her but his head fell back against the bathroom wall.

She stood and rushed into the bedroom.

"Where's the phone?" she screamed, her mind exploding, the room spinning around in her vision. "Where's the—?

"He's dying! And I can't find the phone!"

She fell, hitting the floor with a thud.

"I need to call...to call..." Carla muttered. "I need—"

The phone.

Camouflaged as a fake coconut on the nightstand next to their bed, the lid partially raised.

That must be it! The phone has to be inside, she thought, panic grabbing her.

Her fingers closed around it, and she snatched up the receiver.

She held it against her ear.

No dial tone!

She felt like smashing it to pieces, a sudden burst of rage and frustration overwhelming her.

As she was about to do just that, the hotel's operator said, "We're having trouble with our phone system. Can I help you?"

"An ambulance!" she shouted into the receiver. "My husband may be dying. You've got to hurry!"

"Right away, ma'am," the operator told her.

Carla tossed the receiver aside and stumbled on wobbly legs back toward the bathroom.

Let me help you....

The voice!

"Heal my beloved!" she demanded. "That's what I need you to do. And stop tormenting us!"

A hand.

Then another.

Not on one shoulder this time but *under* both, lifting her up.

Go to him, Carla. Hold him close.

Shaking, afraid to breathe or move or do anything but stay where she was, she knew that she was at the edge of a nervous breakdown.

Do not wait. There is little time left.

She stood for a moment in the middle of the floor, steadying herself, then headed back to the bathroom.

As Carla entered, she gasped.

Kyle was tilted over on his side, shivering in little spasms, his eyelids open a bit as little whimpering sounds escaped his lips. And then he became completely still, quiet, his eyes shut, his face pale, any sign of health and strength gone from it, as though death had already claimed him.

Carla sat beside Kyle, hugging him desperately, trying somehow to keep warmth in his body, and praying to herself that their brief stay on an island paradise had not become another kind of hell.

Part Two

O death, where is thy sting? O grave, where is thy victory?

1 Corinthians 15:55

Chapter Eighteen

*B*oth Carla and Kyle were rushed to a fully staffed clinic near the hotel.

Since his physical state was not immediately apparent to anyone not having his medical records at hand, nothing could be done until tests were performed or Carla regained consciousness and could tell them what she knew.

The couple had been urged to take the precaution of having some type of notification with them, not only to inform doctors of the name of Kyle's condition so that they could treat it but, also, to alert anyone handling him that they should be extraordinarily careful since his bone structure was vulnerable.

But neither Carla nor Kyle ever got around to writing down such details, one of the compromises they had made in the rush to get married with all the other details that were necessary.

Fortunately, the paramedics who put him into the ambulance and those staffers who took over when he arrived at the clinic were gentle enough so that no breakage occurred.

But they had no idea what was wrong.

None had had experience with what afflicted him. Outwardly there was no clue. He seemed quite normal, healthy. His temperature, heart rate and other vital signs were not out of whack.

They felt rather more knowledgeable about Carla.

"Shock..." one of the doctors offered. "She was obviously present when her husband suffered whatever it was that—"

Ever a master of timing, in this case quite accidentally, Carla regained consciousness just then, and a doctor immediately asked her about Kyle.

"We need to know," he pleaded. "Legally and medically, we can't do anything for him until we do."

She told them all the information that she could remember.

The dilemma was not resolved, though, because no one at any of the facilities on Maui could handle what Kyle was suffering.

"He needs to be flown to the mainland," she was told. "We have a helicopter immediately available."

"No..." Carla, still weak, muttered.

"Your husband has to have expert attention."

"I know that!" she exclaimed, summoning the autocratic manner of which she was quite capable.

"Then—"

"Let me speak, doctor. We have a plane waiting for us at the airport."

"A small private plane isn't—"

"This one is neither small nor private. It was supposed to remain the entire week of our honeymoon in case we wanted to be flown elsewhere."

"That sounds horribly expensive."

"I can afford it," she assured him.

The doctor squinted through the thick lenses of his glasses.

"Wait a minute!" he exclaimed. "Yes, of course. Aren't you Carla Gearhart, the country music singer? I was thrown off by the name Carla Rivers."

"I am," she acknowledged. "Amazing, isn't it, what no makeup and a name change can cause."

Carla told him more details about the aircraft, and the doctor admitted that it was probably ideal.

"Now that we are aware of the nature of your husband's condition," he said, "we'll act responsibly. Though we can't treat him here, we can move him properly so that he doesn't have further injury."

"Further injury?" she asked.

"We managed to do some quick X rays. He seems to have broken an astonishing number of bones. But none of these are near his heart and lungs. To that extent, he's very, very fortunate!"

Within half an hour, Kyle had been placed on the former MGM Grand luxury jet, and Carla and he were on their way to Los Angeles.

Chapter Nineteen

As Carla started to perform, memories came back in a flood that threatened to sweep her off the stage but she held on, as though that microphone were her life raft, and refused to do anything but sing from the center of her soul, sing of the love that had transformed her, love from Almighty God and, as well, the handsome young man whom He had been gracious enough to send into her life....

Carla felt some faintness attach itself to her as she headed back to her dressing room after her triumphant time on stage that evening. Her longtime friend and stage manager Albert rushed over to her, and she leaned against him.

"The stress at home," she told him, "and what happened out here."

She pointed toward the stage.

"It was the best ever," he said confidently. "No audience anywhere else has loved you more, Carla."

She grinned halfheartedly as she said, "Hearing that once meant everything to me, you know."

"How right you are. I remember when you would be depressed if a review simply called one of your performances a 'solid' one. Only 'top-notch' or better would satisfy you in those days.''

"I have everything," she said, her voice breaking, "but, Albert, without Kyle I have nothing."

"That's what you think now," he told her, "but—"

"But what?"

"Carla, you aren't the only human being to endure something as bad as this. People get sick. People have cancer. People become paralyzed. This world is afflicted with pain, tragedy, death.''

"Don't...say anymore," she asked.

The backstage area seemed to be spinning out of control, like a child's top suddenly gone haywire, and there she was, in the middle of it.

"What can I do to help you? Anything, Carla," he ventured cautiously.

"Just help me to my dressing room, please. I need to be alone for a little while. If I'm not better in a few minutes, you can call any doctor you want. Deal?"

"Okay...deal," Albert agreed reluctantly, and held her arm as she walked haltingly down the hallway to the star's dressing room at the end.

Once inside, she fell into a well-worn but comfortable easy chair that was resting against one corner.

"God bless you," Albert said as he left.

"You, too, my dear."

She smiled as she added, "I'll be okay. Don't worry."

He shut the door quietly, wondering what he would find if he had to open it again that evening.

Now alone, Carla buried her face in her hands.

My insides, Lord, why are they shaking so much? she thought. *Why—?*

She had to grab the arms of the chair to keep from sliding off.

Kyle is so ill now...if I have to be treated at the hospital tonight, I won't be able to get back home when I hoped.

Tears started their now familiar trek down her cheeks.

When I left, you were—

So pale.

During the three months since they returned from Maui, Kyle would have good days and bad ones, and she allowed herself to fall into the trap of thinking the good days meant that, at last, he was on the way to recovery.

That did not happen.

Kyle would gain ten pounds, then lose more than a dozen, gain five, then lose ten. She inwardly continued her self-deception by celebrating.

That was disturbing enough but then came his moods, ranging from pretty good—optimistic, cheerful in the face of what was happening—to almost an alter ego, the dark side of Kyle Rivers. Those times he would yell at her, would become impatient; and yet these moods did not last very long, though they were in startling contrast to the side of him that she and so many others found irresistible.

"Forgive me...." he would beg her. "The pain is so fierce, Carla."

He need not have asked. She would have forgiven her beloved anything that he conceivably could have done or said.

Carla hired home health care nurses to be at the house twenty-four hours a day. She even paid to have an ambulance on the property day and night, with two paramedics ready to act in an emergency. At her request, Irving Chicolte made the arrangements since she was not able to debate with anyone. Accommodating her meant that the ambulance provider had to realign the schedules for its entire staff, and hire four new men.

But Carla could afford the thousands of dollars a month that all this cost.

"Take it from the petty cash box," she told Irving jokingly.

And, as usual, Irving got her what she wanted. Surprisingly, this came without any kind of battle with those who would have to rearrange their lives, at least the professional part, for whatever length of time necessary.

Fans.

Every paramedic, every nurse was a fan. Their willingness to help was so pronounced that it seemed embarrassing at times, for they waited on Kyle as though their lives depended upon making things as easy as possible for him.

...as easy as possible.

Carla thought of those words as she held a letter in her hands, a letter from a charity dealing with autistic children. Headquartered in Nashville, it was becoming renowned throughout the United States and in various countries across the world, for it had a success rate that was astonishingly high, utilizing a treatment that minimized the use of drugs and maximized two key ingredients: faith and animals. For the people in charge, faith was something that both parents and children needed.

"When the Bible speaks of childlike faith," the founder, Geraldine Andrews, told Carla, "that's all autistic children can have for the foreseeable future. Their minds cannot cope with anything else."

She was smiling while she held a month-old black-and-white kitten.

"For autistic children, childlike faith is coupled with a no-questions-asked, unconditional love," she continued, "the kind that exists between youngsters and their pets. We build on this foundation. While not ignoring complicated but necessary psychological profiles and the like, we do find that, after all the advanced studies and the rest, simplicity in treatment is superior.

"Otherwise, the patient stands a real chance of getting

lost in techniques that have been adopted because some famous doctor somewhere gave them credence that might not be altogether deserved.''

But helping such an organization meant that rehearsals would have to be held nearly forty minutes away from the house, and she could not, at first, bring herself to be as far away as that from Kyle, not when his condition was as vulnerable as it was.

Yet he was the one urging her to go.

"I feel a little better now," he said. "It might be the Lord's timing. I think you're supposed to be helping those kids."

"But you need me more," she protested.

"You have around-the-clock nurses here and an ambulance plus two paramedics on call as well. What could be better than that?"

"What if—?"

"Something happened while you were away?"

"Yes, what if you—?"

"Died, Carla, is that it? That *was* what you were going to say, wasn't it? Sure, that could happen. But, Carla, I'm not going to be alone when that moment comes, whether you're here or not."

She knew what he was going to say, knew it because it had been at the center of her own soul for weeks.

Death...

But not death in and of itself.

She believed as Kyle did, that he was destined for heaven, and that that final journey would not be a frightening one, like running some kind of gauntlet before he made it to the pearly gates at the end.

For him, it would mean release.

For her, it would be another kind of death.

Yet there was something else, connected with death, something that when Kyle said that he was not going to be alone "when that moment comes," he could speak with clarity and assurance.

Kyle was persuasive.

And he got her to agree to do the benefit, but she would hurry home at the end of each day after finishing rehearsals.

It seemed that he was right.

Carla could notice more color in his cheeks, and a steadiness to his voice that she would have thought was no longer possible.

And she told him so.

"I'm happy because you're happy," he told her. "Preparing for this benefit is affecting you. This is good for you, Carla. You're chained to me too much."

"I don't think chained is—"

"All right, that might be too strong. But, remember this— Yes, I'm suffering. I'd be lying to you if I said anything else because you see the truth about me day after day. But as long as I listen to the nurses and do what they say, not much can happen to me. I promise not to go out for golf or tennis!"

He looked at her with an expression she had seen more than once since they first met, and said, "Besides, absence makes the heart grow fonder, remember that?"

"All right, all right," Carla said. "It won't be for more than a couple additional days anyway. I wish you could be there the night of the benefit itself."

Kyle wished he could go anywhere she did. But his mobility was steadily decreasing. The problem was a singular one: his nervous system was less and less able to serve his body efficiently. An increasing numbness could make otherwise simple injuries far more serious because they might go unnoticed.

Even his wheelchair had to be especially constructed, with extra thick foam padding at the back and on the seat itself.

He seldom left the house.

Within it, his environment could be carefully controlled but the outside world seldom provided such opportunities. He could not go to church so Carla arranged to have the service videotaped by her own production crew. This worked out so well that the top Christian TV network asked if they could telecast it over the stations that carried their programming. Carla and Kyle were happy to oblige.

Her not inconsiderable wealth allowed him other advantages that were far from commonplace, including a screening room that was every bit as plush as any Hollywood motion picture studio had. Kyle invited friends over from the Nashville area and, also, quite a group drove in periodically from Winslow Christian College. Films seen in what was essentially a miniature theater was one of the highlights of their visit, with Irving Chicolte responsible for obtaining video copies long before any were released to stores, and in some cases, before films had left their theatrical showings.

"In some ways, things are so good," Kyle said, typically minimizing the progressive nature of his condition to the point where it would seem, by his manner, that a cure was just around the corner.

At first Carla chalked this up to denial which, she thought, for Kyle was far more pervasive than with most people. But then she stumbled upon another explanation, one that sent her away in tears until she had had time to sit down and think about what she had overheard that afternoon five months after he collapsed at the hotel in Maui.

Kyle was not denying the truth...he was reaching beyond it...making contact with another reality altogether.

Chapter Twenty

Kyle was sitting in the midst of the rose garden, which was more lush as each week passed.

And talking.

"Yes, I know," she heard him saying, a remarkable peace in his voice. "That's really wonderful."

Carla was going to go outside and ask him who he was talking to but stopped.

"Yes, it will be wonderful," he went on. "I wish you could tell me more but I know you can't. Language can only convey so much. I'll have to wait for the experience itself to fully appreciate—"

He bowed his head, and it seemed he was sobbing.

That was when Carla decided she would have to go out and—

A hand again, resting ever so gently on her shoulder.

Stay, dear lady. This moment is not for you. That time will be later, yours and yours alone.

Carla protested.

"But he may need me now!" she exclaimed. "He's crying."

Are there only tears of sorrow? Would you rob him of this joy even as pain races through his body?

She swung around, hoping to confront that which she herself had never seen.

Kyle was speaking again.

Carla faced the sliding glass door again.

"I wish—" he said.

Go ahead, Kyle.

Behind her, that same voice, as before, but this time it seemed to be speaking to both of them.

"I wish Carla could know how I feel," he continued.

She will, Kyle. She will know as you do this very moment.

He started coughing, and she could tell that he was seriously hurting.

"I can't stand seeing her grief," he said. "She tries to hide it but some of it gets past her outward smile. She is acting as though I have already been taken away."

The voice was even softer, kinder, sweeter than in the past.

That, too, will change, Kyle.

He could not understand.

"How can I comprehend what you are trying to tell me?" he asked. "Carla will go to pieces. There is no more to it than that."

He reached upward, toward the heavens.

"Take me now, Lord," he begged with great passion. "Don't prolong this nightmare for Carla. As desperately as I want to live an extra minute, an hour, longer than that, I know that every moment I *am* given is that much more uncertainty for my beloved, making her wonder when it *will* finally happen.

"Oh, I know she is trying so hard to prepare herself, sobbing as she does until her insides must ache, thinking that I can't hear her when she does this, not wanting me ever to know that, in a way, some part of her is dying, too.''

Carla could endure no more. She pulled back from the door, and walked toward the stairs, reaching them only to fall against the banister.

''Help me!'' she cried out.

Right now you must deny yourself and help Kyle. He wants to die, Carla. Say something to him.

She stood, raising a fist at the high ceiling.

''Can you blame the guy?'' she declared angrily. ''He has had enough. *Can't you see that?*''

The voice responded in an instant.

Go to Kyle, put your arms around him.

Carla inhaled sharply. She glanced at her arms.

''Oh, Lord, I want to hold him forever, and never let go! This isn't fair. We had one night together.''

No hand on her shoulder, no gossamer touch of reassurance.

Just that voice, just a few more words, directly into her brain.

Go, Carla, spend the time with him. There is so little left.

She started toward the glass door which she could see at the end of a hallway.

Frames on the wall.

Along its entire length on both sides.

Some around gold records. Some featuring her and major film stars. A whole group taken during her Oscar night of triumph.

And then, near the end, shots of her and Kyle, shots which she had intended to add to during the coming years.

I was going to take him all over the world, she thought. *We were going to see a dozen countries, hold each other in candlelight, moonlight, the bright sun glistening off our tanned bodies on black sand beaches.*

Now—

She saw him through the glass door.

So pale looking...like an increasingly helpless child... that once strong, firm body gone...in its place—

She opened the door slowly, and walked up to him.

"There's little time," he said.

"I know."

"Help me into bed. We can lie down together, we can—"

He was fighting tears but not very successfully.

"Oh, Carla, I just want to feel you next to me."

She grabbed the handles of the wheelchair. As they left the rose garden, the scent of many blossoms followed them.

"The best year..." she muttered. "Never more beautiful, never sweeter."

Kyle could not speak, and he was breathing heavily.

She managed to get the wheelchair on the lift she had had installed but it was slow and she was upstairs before it was.

As she waited, the voice spoke but more briefly than before.

The best year, Carla, remember that.

She did not want Kyle to hear her so she spoke barely above a whisper.

"For the roses maybe!" she said.

Minutes later, she was able to get Kyle off the wheelchair and onto the bed, but regretting that she had given the household staff the night off.

Then Carla crawled in under the covers, and pressed her body up against his, their sides touching as though they were Siamese twins joined at the hips. They went to sleep like that, the two of them, dreading the coming dawn.

Carla dared not move.

She had fully expected those hours together with Kyle to be the last they would have, and for a while, she fought sleep, rebelled against it because of it being the intruder robbing her of awareness, awareness that the man she loved was beside her, and that as long as she could feel his body, as long as she sensed his warmth mingling with her own, he would not be taken from her, would not grow cold and hard and lifeless.

The night had passed. Morning light was filtering in through the gossamer-thin curtains that hung over the large window near their bed.

"Kyle..." she asked cautiously, her voice trembling. "My dear, how are you this morning?"

No response.

Her heart seemed to stop beating.

Lord, Lord, don't let it be now, she prayed. *I...I'm not ready yet. Please, don't let it come so soon.*

A sound.

Breathing.

She held her breath, thinking that it might be her own.

Still there.

She turned her head slowly, to look at Kyle, to see—

He was looking at her, a weak smile on his face.

"I slept straight through," he said.

Carla smiled instinctively, rejoicing, until she saw his eyes.

Bloodred, except for the pupils.

He saw her expression.

"What's wrong?" he asked but as soon as he had spoken, he closed his eyes again, and seemed on the verge of passing out, then opened them again, adding, "Sorry, Carla. I felt some pain then but it's gone now. I feel better, God knows I feel better."

She wanted to reach out and hug him but knew she could no longer do even that, so she gently took his left hand in her own, and held it like that.

"Your hand is so soft," he told her. "I could hold it forever and never want to let go."

"I'll stay here as long as you want," Carla said.

"But the benefit's tonight. Don't you need to get there early, run through the numbers one more time?"

"I can let that go. We know the songs so well. A little more rehearsal won't change anything. I'll call everyone, and tell them when to get to the arena."

"Are you sure?" Kyle asked. "Those children will need whatever money you can raise. You need to be your best."

"I will be my best if I can spend as much time with you today as possible," Carla assured him.

He nodded slowly.

"Okay..." he said. "What do you want to do?"

"Just sit here, talk," she told him. "That's all I want."

"I'd like to see the horses."

"But, Kyle—"

"With the paramedics helping, I can do it," he added. "There's some risk, of course, but I stay here in this one room every minute of every hour of each day. The greater risk is that I will go crazy."

She tried to resist, realizing how close to death he seemed just hours before, but then it became clear how much he wanted to get outside.

Lord, what if I don't let him, she thought, *and he dies tonight? How will I feel then?*

By seven-fifteen, the paramedics were back on the property after spending the night off at their own homes. After breakfast, while a morning mist hung over the land, they were lifting Kyle out of bed and into the wheelchair.

"See!" he proclaimed. "It's working out fine."

It was good to see him happy.

Lord, thank you, she prayed. *Lord, thank you so much.*

Once outside, the paramedics wheeled him toward the stables which were near the opposite end of the property.

"Can you get Black Lightning ready?" Kyle asked.

"Ready?" she replied, alarmed.

He was chuckling as he told her, "Not to ride, Carla. I just want to see him, to run my hand along his side."

She nodded, and walked ahead, to tell the stable boy what she wanted. In a few minutes, the sleek mare was standing in front of Kyle, and seemed to recognize him, for she leaned down and licked him on the cheek.

Kyle wrinkled up his nose.

"She has an upset stomach," he said. "Her breath is worse than usual."

The stable boy assured him that Black Lightning would be given the right medicine. If that did not correct her condition, a vet would be summoned.

"I love her," Kyle said. "We had some great times riding from one end of this place to the other."

He started to cry, in front of the paramedics, and was embarrassed but could not help himself.

One of the men, the youngest, was named Andrew, and he placed a hand lightly on Kyle's shoulder.

"Men cry," he said with great sympathy, "it's not weak or feminine to do this."

"How did you know?"

"You are an easy man to get to know, Mr. Rivers. After all that you've been through, are a few tears wrong?"

"No..." Kyle admitted. "Thank you...thank you for saying that."

"It came from my heart, sir."

After staying there with Black Lightning for another few minutes, Kyle acknowledged that he was becoming tired. So, he was returned to the house, and taken upstairs to bed where he fell asleep almost immediately.

Chapter Twenty-One

The voices of a million angels could not express my gratitude. All that I am, and ever hope to be, I owe it all to Thee....

Carla Gearhart Rivers sat in the back seat of her prized British limo. She tried to relax, to be secure in the knowledge that nothing had happened to Kyle while she was at the arena.

During a break in her performance, she was able to call home on her cell phone and talked to him directly.

So weak.... she thought. So very weak.

But he was alert and looking forward to her coming back. She told him that the evening was going really well, and said that she loved him.

She called a second time, after the show was over, and she was heading toward the exit. Her maid told her that Kyle seemed fine, that he had to go to sleep but she checked on him minutes before the call and he was resting comfortably.

Carla thanked her, breathed a sigh of relief, and within five minutes was on the way back home.

"It may take a bit longer," Rocco Gilardi warned.

"Why?" she asked.

"Fog is moving in. It may be thick in spots."

She glanced out the side window, noticed the first few puffs of it.

"Do your best," she replied.

"For you, nothing less than that."

Carla smiled, then closed her eyes and tried to calm herself down.

She was still hyper after that performance.

In the audience were several of the children being treated at the center. They seemed to come out of the strange insular world that autism forced them into, and for a couple of hours, seemed happy.

Nothing else was on her calendar for the next several weeks. She and Kyle could spend every minute together.

Her eyelids shot open, and she felt herself suddenly drenched with perspiration over every inch of her body.

...for the next several weeks.

Carla gasped because she knew that there might be only days left, or less. After all, while Kyle was strong, how much longer could that strength keep him going?

*Someday...*she started thinking...*I might have to face seeing him down to a hundred pounds or less, according to what the medical report mentioned. Or I could be away from him, on an errand or whatever else, for a few hours and, then, find him...*

The fog was thicker.

But her driver convincingly assured her that there would be no problem, that she had nothing to worry about.

"Should I call the house?" she speculated. "Should I tell my husband that we might be late?"

"No, ma'am," the driver said. "we're going to—"

He slammed on the brakes, nearly throwing Carla off the seat.

"What is it?" she asked.

An accident ahead.

"They aren't as fortunate," he told her. "Might have been their brakes. Shall I stop to see what we can do to help?"

Carla hesitated, torn between wanting to get home to be with Kyle, and stopping to offer whatever assistance they could give.

"Stop," she said. "Someone might be injured."

Both Carla and the driver got out and hurried to the car ahead, which appeared to have run off the road into a ditch beside it.

Two bodies inside.

"There's no blood," the driver noted. "Yet—"

In an instant the two men in the front seat moved, one of them carrying a very large revolver.

"Step aside!" they said in unison.

"Run, ma'am," Carla's driver said. "Get back to the car. Drive away!"

"I can't," she said. "I can't—"

The man, slighter than the other, on the driver's side swung the door open, knocking Rocco Gilardi off his feet.

They struggled briefly until the other man hit the driver with the handle of his revolver. Gilardi staggered but did not fall. He lunged for the other man, started to swing him around just as the one with the revolver fired, hitting Gilardi in the chest.

"You could have gotten me!" protested the smaller man.

"Could haves don't amount to—" the other man shouted.

"The broad! She's getting away."

Realizing she could do nothing, Carla had started to run seconds before and was nearly at the Bentley.

"Shoot her!" the smaller man demanded. "She's a famous star, I think. She could get all the media to cooperate. They'd find us in no time. *Shoot the broad now!*"

The man with the revolver turned, aimed it at Carla just as she was opening the door. He missed, shattering the window instead.

"Again! Don't miss this time!"

Carla managed to get the limo started, and slammed her foot down hard against the accelerator.

Another bullet hit the hood.

Frustrated, angry, the smaller man grabbed the revolver from his partner and waited until Carla was close enough for him to see her form through the front windshield.

He aimed, aimed more expertly.

And fired!

The bullet hit her in the shoulder with such force that she was thrown back against the seat, the steering wheel ripped from her fingers, her prized Bentley now barreling ahead until it careened into a telephone poll up the road, bursting into flames upon impact.

She was able to get out but her clothes were aflame and she could not run very far, dropping just a few yards from the two men, while writhing in agony.

The smaller man walked calmly up to Carla Gearhart Rivers and pointed his revolver at her.

She felt something familiar as death seemed to be swooping in upon her.

A hand.

It had not simply rested in a comforting manner on her shoulder this time but was lifting her up, with exquisite gentleness, no words spoken or needed between her and the sublimely beautiful being she now saw, only the momentarily distant beating of ten thousand upon ten thousand pairs of wings heard, like a rising gossamer serenade bidding her welcome, and, in that instant when time was no more, Carla Gearhart suddenly thought she would have to say goodbye to everything and everyone that she had ever known.

Chapter Twenty-Two

Kyle expected Carla home soon.

He was not so much possessive but dependent. The degree to which he needed her was increasing day by day.

As his condition seemed to worsen over the past weeks, his patience deteriorated, and that night was no exception.

But Kyle had a good reason: he wanted to look his best.

To do that, he needed help, however demeaning this was, help which the paramedics were happy to provide.

Kyle could not stand by himself, and he asked one of them to hold him at the washbasin so that he could shave. He was able to lift the lightweight razor well enough and move it around his face but he needed to do so with care, since his grip was not tight, and he might cut himself if his hand wavered.

But the shaving was completed without any nicking.

"Do I look a little less ugly?" he asked.

Both men were tall, strong. One was named Ted Bernstein, in his midthirties, bald, thin-faced, square-jawed; the other, Charlie Swinton, barely beyond college age, still possessed hair so abundant that he had to wear it long whether he wanted to or not.

"Charlie, that's one mean crop," Kyle observed.

"Yeah, I know, I've had to work with it all my life. But that's better than not having any."

He winked at his partner who showed mock offense.

"You know the reason I'm bald?" Ted asked.

"Have no idea," Kyle told him.

"My brain's getting bigger, smarter, keeps pushing the roots out!"

The three of them had a good laugh over that.

It was now time for Kyle to change his clothes, which presented some real problems. He could barely move any of his limbs, so into a fresh shirt and slacks meant some pain and not a little danger.

"I can break my arm or my leg like some old dry twig," he muttered.

Charlie winced.

"Now that you mention it," he said, "I gotta ask you something."

"Go ahead…"

"You believe in God, right?"

"I sure do."

"And you have no doubt at all that He is merciful and full of grace, as an old hymn says?" Charlie asked.

"Right again."

"Then why has He allowed you, of all people, to have the problems that you endure day after day?"

"You said 'of all people'? What did you mean by that?"

"A devout man, someone whose career of singing also carries with it a ministry through song."

"And the chance to witness onstage!"

"Exactly," Charlie continued, "you only aggravate what I'm thinking."

"That God should be treating me better than He seems to be doing?"

"Well, yes, that's what I was getting at. Now, I don't mean any offense."

"None taken. God is the author of truth. And you are seeking the truth through your skepticism."

"Then what's the answer? The wicked often get off scot-free, and the righteous carry a heavy burden of tragedy. How can that be? Better stated, *why* is it?"

"I'm not a theologian," Kyle started to say, "but I have to look at myself, and my situation, and tell you that God still loves me."

"If I treated my son the way God has been treating you, I would be accused of child abuse."

"The fact that I'm dying?"

Charlie hesitated, not having intended to be as straightforward as that.

"Go ahead," Kyle urged him. "Do you think that I can be upset by *anything* at this stage?"

"I suppose not. But to someone such as myself, God seems the opposite of kind and loving."

"I've got an example of a situation that a friend of mine at Winslow College told me. It really happened."

"Go ahead."

"This man's son was in a commuter plane crash. It looked at first as though he would be one of the few survivors. But then he took a turn for the worse. The father prayed and prayed and prayed that his boy would pull through."

Kyle's expression turned even more serious.

"He did, Charlie. The son pulled through."

"How old was the kid?"

"Fifteen."

"Great. That's a real example of the grace you were talking about. Chalk one up for God."

"No..."

"No? The kid survived. The father got his son back."

"That's what it seems, right?"

"What else could I think?"

"That's the beginning of the story."

"A great beginning!"

"But a lousy ending. In college, this man's son got into drugs, became a pusher, got AIDS from an infected needle, and died horribly, within a period of just under three years. He went from a robust 175 pounds to 87."

Charlie was silent, emotionally overwhelmed.

"Would it not have been better for the boy to have perished in that plane crash?" Kyle offered. "That would not have been the tragedy that his survival became. Can you see where I'm heading?"

Finally Charlie was able to say something.

"You think God can tell the future, then?" he asked.

"I *know* it," Kyle replied. "The Bible says it, therefore I believe it."

"And you're saying that what we call tragedies could be something else if we knew what was going to happen a year, two, five years from now?"

"That's exactly what I'm saying. There are matters in this life that only faith can handle," he said.

"You're evading the issue."

"Yes, I am, because I don't have the answer. And there seems to be no immediate answer. I have nothing left but faith when that happens, you know. But at least faith enables me to get through each day."

"Faith that God isn't stabbing you, a faithful man, in the back?"

"It goes much deeper than that, Charlie. It—"

As they waited in the master bedroom, Kyle thought he heard the front doorbell ringing downstairs twice. The maid and other household staff members always had each evening off, except when a dinner party was scheduled, so Ted Bernstein said that he would see who was outside.

"It couldn't be Carla," Kyle thought. "She has a key."

They waited until Ted returned. When he did, he seemed nervous, unable at first to look directly at anyone.

Then, sighing, he sat down on the bed next to Kyle who asked expectantly, "Where's Carla?"

"Mr. Rivers...I...I...have to tell you something," Ted said slowly.

"Carla's been delayed? What a shame! She could have had someone call, though. When will she be home?"

The paramedic had to form each word with care, forcing it out as though his vocal chords were partially paralyzed.

"Your wife is very seriously hurt...." he added.

What the other man was saying failed to register at first with Kyle, who stared blankly at him.

"What in the world are you saying?" Kyle asked, hearing the words but not comprehending.

"It happened during a robbery attempt on the way home," Ted Bernstein spoke. "It happened—"

"How?"

"Shot."

"Where?"

"Mrs. Rivers was—" the paramedic started to say, his eyes filling with tears.

"I want to know. I *have* to know."

"Your wife was shot in a robbery attempt on the way home," the paramedic told him. "Just half a dozen miles from here."

"How?"

"It was horrible, Mr. Rivers. Don't make me tell you now!"

"When? An hour from now? A day? Next week? Never? Is that what you're trying to do? Never let me know!"

"She was...shot."

"Where?"

"Must I—?"

"Yes! Where was my wife shot?"

"In the back, Mr. Rivers. She's alive...but the doctor's don't expect her to survive surgery."

Kyle started shaking with rage and sorrow.

"Take me to her!" he demanded. *"I want to be with Carla. I want to—"*

He tried frantically to get out of bed but the two paramedics gently restrained him and Kyle managed to raise both hands upward, crying out, "My God, my God, why? My God...Carla!!!"

He glanced from one man to the other.

"Where is she now?" he asked, desperation choking him. "Where have they taken my beloved?"

Both paramedics hesitated, well aware that whatever either said could have a significant impact upon whether he lived or died, and they tried to be evasive but Kyle would not let them continue.

"I demand to know," he told him. "You have no right to keep the truth from me. I am not a child who has to be coddled."

Ted Bernstein nodded with obvious reluctance and said, "In surgery at Nashville Memorial, Mr. Rivers."

Abruptly Kyle fell forward, against the two paramedics. *"No!"*

That was to be the last time Kyle Rivers screamed that night.

A second later, he was able to gather enough strength from a largely depleted inner reservoir to push past the two paramedics, catching both by surprise, and started to walk to the bedroom door and into the hallway outside.

After just less than two feet, he tripped and fell, hitting the floor hard.

He should have died.

He did not.

Chapter Twenty-Three

*K*yle Rivers had to be rushed to Nashville Memorial Hospital where a team of doctors waited to treat him.

This time it seemed that there would be no last minute recovery, no way for even the wisdom of renowned specialists to save his life.

Carla was only two doors down the corridor from where Kyle had been placed. She had been able to kick out with her legs and catch the assailant off balance, giving her a second or two to get to her feet and start to run, thinking desperately that surely no one would shoot a woman in the back.

Wrong.

She was very wrong.

He fired once.

The bullet hit her in the back, right at the middle of her spine.

Carla went down immediately but had enough self-control to pretend that she was dead. The assailant nudged her with his foot but when she did not groan or make any other sound, he lost interest.

It was less than fifteen minutes before an ambulance and two State Police cars arrived but to Carla, the wait, as she drifted in and out of consciousness, seemed vastly longer.

Yet there was little pain.

And that meant she could worry about something awful, praying with growing desperation that she was wrong.

"Am I paralyzed, Lord?" she spoke out loud at one point. *"Am I—?"*

Chapter Twenty-Three

Part Three

All we know
Of what they do above,
Is that they happy are,
and that they love!

Theodore Tilton

Chapter Twenty-Four

"*I am astonished!*"

A strange voice, unrecognized.

The suddenness of the voice jolted him, a voice that seemed to be coming from a great distance.

"*I feel the same way. He should not be alive. Or else so badly off that death would seem the greatest of mercies.*"

Another voice, equally far away.

"*Please stop chattering away, whoever you are,*" he begged. "*Where is my beloved? Where have you—?*"

He needed Carla. He wanted Carla. He could not go on without her.

"*Do you have any idea if Kyle Rivers knows what happened?*"

"*Yes, he does. He learned minutes before he tripped and lost consciousness.*"

"*Can you blame him? They seemed so happy together. That would be enough to squelch the will to live in any other man.*"

"*Under other circumstances, with anybody else, I would agree but this guy's not so ordinary.*"

"Physically speaking, sure, you're right on the money."

"It's more than just that."

"What do you mean?"

"It has to be this young man's spirit. It seems to give him a measure of strength that is comprised of more than flesh and bones."

"Can you quantify that medically?"

"I can't."

"Then what sense does such speculation make?"

"Ever the professional skeptic! Let's put it this way—if he survives, it makes a great deal of sense, wouldn't you say?"

Silence then.

The voices faded.

Pain.

A great deal of it, vast submerging waves of pain that seemed endless, unstoppable, unendurable.

And then someone's face in the distance, coming closer.

He recognized it.

"Carla, my love!" he shouted. *"I knew it wasn't true. I knew they were surely wrong. Let me hold you. Let me—"*

Gone.

The face had vanished.

He was alone in a bleak abyss, no more voices, not a face to be seen, nothingness so encompassing that it seemed—

Eternal.

He reached out.

"Where is heaven, Lord?" he cried.

There was no answer.

Not then, anyway.

Chapter Twenty-Five

During the first few hours of treatment, Carla had been close to death, so close in fact that her doctors had not given her any chance to live, as a result of trauma to her body and exposure, but one other factor especially.

Blood loss.

If another five minutes or less had passed before help arrived, she would not have survived.

But as with Kyle, doctors were amazed at her strength.

"Anyone else would be dead by now," one of them said.

"Not this woman. She's special, really special."

In the meantime, those who loved her could only wait....

Roxie Chicolte sat in the waiting room on the floor where Kyle was eventually taken, and she was crying hysterically.

Irving was not accustomed to seeing her doing this, the hard-as-nails facade evaporated.

"I'm crying for two," she said dramatically, "for Carla and for me. You can do what you want."

"I wonder about Kyle...if she...if Carla—" he started to add, then turned away.

Roxie heard little sounds coming from him.

"Dear, are you—?" she asked.

He did not turn around as he answered.

"Crying? Yes, I'm crying, Roxie. Is that a crime? You think you're the only one who can?"

Roxie reached out for him, and they hugged each other, acting like two teenagers who had just encountered the greatest tragedy of their lives.

"What if she lives and...and is only a vegetable," she mused between sobs. "Kyle can't care for her. They both will need assistance around the clock."

"Thank God that—" he started to say, then self-consciously added, "In a manner of speaking, of course, thank God that the money will never run out."

It was not the money, however, that most concerned Roxie.

"If Carla is disabled in any way, how can she endure that burden plus what is going on with Kyle?" she spoke a few seconds later. "That dear soul's gone through so much before this, and now, again!"

Death so close, like a phantom night, cold and cruel....

They both were feeling scared just then, and strangely lonely, as though Carla and Kyle were already gone.

"How nice it would be to pray about now," Roxie muttered.

"Don't start," he growled, "don't ever start!"

Death so close...

Kyle himself tottered on the brink of it so many times during the next few hours at Nashville Memorial that no one could have kept count, his blood pressure falling precipitously, his heart rate fluttering.

Only the machines...

That was what most of the doctors would concur was keeping Carla and Kyle Rivers alive.

"Turn off everything," they undoubtedly would say, "and neither could pull through. They're too weak."

With some irony, the machines each were hooked to turned out to be either identical or similar, both fighting for survival. Wires and tubes to his body were part of the process of measuring the obvious—heart rate, blood pressure, the rest—but they could not detect anything of the emotions, the spirit, the soul, and it was there that a tug-of-war of sorts was being fought, Kyle wanting to be by Carla's side, and wondering if she would die anytime soon, and how much he wanted to die with her. But something else was tugging him in the opposite direction, pulling him away from eternity and back to mortality, away from what his Bible had been promising before mortal life since he was old enough to understand it, and returning him to a world filled with suffering, pain all over his body, weakness in every limb, no ability any longer to take care of his most basic bodily functions without the help of a paid attendant, however efficient and courteous. A world that could soon be without Carla Gearhart Rivers, who would have been his only reason for fighting to keep hold of that imperfect, anguish-ridden life, and yet there he was, clinging to a flesh-and-blood existence, a voice coming from some distant place, a voice that said, "Not yet, Kyle. Not yet. Hang on. You will understand soon because your Lord will give you the clearest, brightest vision you have ever had…no more seeing through a glass darkly."

A group was gathering outside, dozens of men, women and children, right in front of the entrance to Nashville Memorial.

At first they looked like typical Carla Gearhart Rivers fans, and some were precisely that, but most had come for another reason, from Kyle's church and elsewhere, people who had come in contact with either or both of them, people who shared their faith, people who knew that if they

died, they would simply shed their flesh-and-blood bodies
and live eternally, the finite becoming infinite, the perish-
able becoming incorruptible, life no longer measured in
terms of seconds, minutes, hours, days, weeks and years
but then without measurement, spent in the presence of the
Father, Son and Holy Spirit forever.

And yet—

"We pray, Heavenly Father," they spoke as a group,
"that if it be Thy will, these two fine believers, so devoted,
so loving, be allowed to tarry for a while with the rest of
us. We are enriched by their presence, Lord God Jehovah,
and we know the blessings they can bring to others.

"If You let them live, it will be, we pray from the center
of our own souls, to Your honor, to Your glory, their witness for Thee spreading beyond this building, this city, this
state."

A dozen or more men and women were crying in the
midst of that prayer, and perhaps because of it, emotions
springing forth without shame, without any concern for
what others would think.

"Oh, Lord, Lord, Lord..." the prayer continued, "we
will be here throughout the night and whatever part of the
day necessary until we hear what happens. It may be that
our wishes are not Yours, that our hope is not what Your
Will permits. If so, tell them that our love for them will
never die, and that we look forward to that blessed reunion
You have promised in Your holy, inerrant, infallible and
inspired Word."

And so it went that night and into the morning.

Chapter Twenty-Six

Every so often the words from outside would reach Carla and Kyle as nurses opened the windows in their respective rooms.

"If they're aware at all, if they understand anything," one nurse suggested, *"it must help them to know that there is so much love out there."*

So much love...

They heard parts of prayers during parts of scattered moments when consciousness returned like a will-o'-the-wisp apparition; they heard, and the sounds of those voices seemed like the singing of ten thousand angels....

Kyle opened his eyes, and saw Roxie sitting in a metal chair next to the bed.

"Are...you...an...angel?" he asked.

"Are you drunk?" she retorted.

"Drugged, I guess."

"Thought so."

"Let me hug you, Roxie."

"You shouldn't be moving at all. I'll get a doctor."

"No, don't, just let me hug you."

"You almost died last night. Your strength is—"

"I know."

"You know?"

"Yes, Roxie, I know. I don't *think* I know, I didn't *imagine* it, but I felt it very strongly."

"What did you feel?" she asked, holding her breath momentarily.

"God."

Roxie held her peace, having enough sense to know that that was not the time for any theological argument.

"I felt Him everywhere, dear, dear friend. I felt Him calling to me, calling me to His eternal kingdom."

"What happened?"

"It was because of Carla. I knew that if she survived, it would be so awful for her without me. I knew that if I did not die just then, I would hate to go on living without her. But how could I pray that we both would die? How could I ask my God to take my beloved, to take that beautiful life from her?"

Roxie fought tears, fought them desperately, but they would come just the same as Kyle continued.

"So I begged the Creator of the universe, of every living thing, I begged Him to spare us, to let us go on living this mortal life, until later, until we were old, and ready, ready to be lifted from bodies no longer of any use, to be taken past the gates of heaven into His presence."

It was Kyle's turn to weep.

"I saw God smile," he told Roxie the atheist. "I saw Him smile, and I heard Him say, 'You *will* live, and your beloved *will* live, and I shall wait.'"

Kyle's voice was becoming weaker.

"Roxie, Roxie, I saw, praise His holy name, I...I saw standing next to Him a radiant Jesus, I saw Him by His Father's side, and it was beautiful, and I knew my faith, as I knew Carla's faith would never be in vain, that we believed what was *real*, oh, Roxie, that's right, everything was real, and...and—''

He smiled weakly but sweetly.

"I must sleep now," he whispered. "I must—"

She bent over the bed and he reached out and pressed one hand at the back of her neck, squeezing his fingers partially around it.

"That's...all...I...can...say," he told her. "I need to rest. Forgive me, Roxie, I am so tired now."

"It's enough, what you have told me," Roxie assured him, "it's something that I've been—"

"Praying for?" he asked, his voice almost gone.

"—hoping for," she added, blushing a bit.

In a moment he closed his eyes.

"Goodbye, dearest Roxie," he told her. "Goodbye for now."

Hours later, after Roxie had left the room, and Irving had taken her place, it was time for her to go back in again.

"Would you get me some coffee?" she asked.

"Sure."

"Was he okay?"

At first Irving did not answer.

"Was he—?" she repeated.

"More than okay."

"What do you mean?"

"Humming."

"Humming? What was he humming?"

"Some hymn. I had no idea what it was, so I asked a couple of nurses to come in, hoping he wouldn't have stopped by then."

"Did they recognize the hymn?"

"One of them did. She said it was called 'Fairest Lord Jesus.'"

"Oh..."

Irving left to get the coffee, his mind swirling with the way Kyle had been responding. Every so often, he had walked down the corridor to Carla's room. He decided to do so now and as he approached the doorway, he heard her humming as well.

"Nurse…" he spoke to one who happened to be passing by.

"Yes, sir?"

"That's a hymn, isn't it?"

"Yes, it is."

His throat muscles were tightening up.

"Is it called 'Fairest Lord Jesus'?" he asked.

She listened more carefully for a moment, then, smiling, told him, "Yes, sir, I believe it is. One of my grandmother's favorites. She would sit on the front porch in her rocking chair, and hum the melody or sing the words without worrying about anyone hearing her. But people passing by *did* hear, and they would stop and listen, for my grandmother had a beautiful voice, you know. She always said, during those final days, that she was not singing to please people but singing to please her Lord."

Irving thanked her, and forgetting the coffee briefly, stood in the doorway, waiting until Carla had finished, then he hurried back down the corridor, and reentered Kyle's room, dropping both cups.

"My God!" he said, startled.

Awake.

Kyle was awake though Roxie had momentarily fallen asleep.

Kyle turned his head and glanced at him.

"Sorry…" Irving apologized. "Bad habit."

"Very…bad," muttered Kyle.

Irving excused himself and hurried down the corridor outside to the nurses' station at the end.

Less than a minute passed before a doctor was racing to the private room that Kyle had been granted.

As the two men entered, neither of them was anywhere near prepared for what they would see.

Kyle...

Now sitting up in bed, waiting for them, holding Roxie's hand.

"I'm going to beat this thing," he announced triumphantly. "Carla would want me to do that, of course...and I'm not about to disappoint my beloved."

He looked at them.

"She's still alive, isn't she?" he asked uncertainly.

"Two doors down," Roxie told him, her voice trembling because she hoped that he would not ask her to spell out Carla's condition.

"How is she doing?"

"We don't know yet."

Kyle looked at her intently, trying to perceive whether or not she was hiding anything from him.

"What *aren't* you telling me?" he asked pointedly.

"Kyle..."

"Tell me."

"You're still so weak. We thought you...you might be—"

"Dead by now?" he interrupted.

"Yes...."

"I still want to know. Don't hold anything back."

Roxie glanced helplessly at Irving.

"You want me to tell him?" he asked.

She nodded, a grim expression on her face.

Irving turned to Kyle and muttered, "I'm not comfortable doing this right now of all times."

"I'm the one who's got tubes stuck in him, and monitors analyzing every part of my body. Don't talk to me about being uncomfortable, dear friend."

"All right," Irving agreed, clearing his throat rather theatrically. "Good news first or the bad. It's your call."

"Good news."

"There's no doubt that Carla's going to live. Her vital signs are stabilized. And she probably will be returning to full consciousness soon, if all continues to go well. She is half alert every so often but completely out of it other times. She was asking about you whenever she could talk at all."

"That's wonderful. Praise Jesus!"

Irving looked away from him.

"The bad news, Irving...what's the bad news?"

Irving tried to tell him but could not as he started to sob.

"Carla may never walk again!" Roxie blurted out. "She seems to be paralyzed from the waist down."

Lord, help us pull through this, Kyle prayed to himself a few minutes later after the Chicoltes had left to get some breakfast. *You've been gracious enough to provide so many miracles over the past few months, I...I don't know if it's right that I ask for another. But I guess I have, Lord, because if Carla is to be in a wheelchair for the rest of her life, I need the strength to shoulder my own burdens and to help her at the same time. It can't be in my strength but it has to be in Yours or everything will fail, and the two of us will live lives only of misery day after day.*

He was not sure what to say next, so he held his hands out, palms upward and raised them toward the ceiling.

What else should I put before You this day, blessed One? he continued. *Is there something else that I should say? If not, then please, precious Jesus, take this burden upon Your shoulders and—*

Not realizing that Kyle was near the end of a prayer, a doctor barged into the room, then stopped.

"Sorry to interrupt," he said. "Your wife is conscious now. Is there anything you want me to tell her?"

"I will tell her myself, Doctor," Kyle replied a bit sternly. "Please help me into that wheelchair."

"You're in no condition to get out of bed."

"God will take care of the rest."

"I don't believe in God."

Kyle was tempted to witness for faith to the man then and there but decided to wait until later.

Give me the opportunity, Lord, he prayed quickly. *Let me be Your instrument in reaching through to this man's soul.*

"I don't believe in taxes but I still pay them."

"So does everyone else," the doctor retorted.

"But countless thousands of people do try to avoid this."

"It's not the same."

"But it's good enough for me."

"I will *not* allow you out of bed."

"I will *not* allow you to stop me."

"Mr. Rivers, two nights ago, you were nearly dead."

"Two nights from now, I could *be* dead. What if I never got to see Carla again as a result of waiting too long?"

"I understand what you're saying, Mr. Rivers. I am not completely bereft of emotion, you know."

"I won't let you stop me."

"I have no choice but to give you a sedative."

Momentarily he stepped out into the corridor, and asked a nurse to get him what he needed.

Only a few seconds passed until he was in the room again, *and yet he saw Kyle standing on his feet, and inching over to the wheelchair!*

"That's impossible!" the doctor exclaimed uncomprehendingly. "You were in miserable condition before."

"I may still be in miserable condition, as you say, but

nothing will stand in the way of a chance to see my beloved.''

The doctor hesitated.

"How deeply you love her!" he said.

"As much as life itself!"

"Mr. Rivers, forgive me. I'll help you."

A minute later, he was wheeling Kyle down to Carla's room.

She was sitting up in bed.

"What a mess we are!" she exclaimed but Kyle knew her well enough to see that she was hiding her physical anguish behind a cheerful facade.

The doctor left the wheelchair on the right side of her bed.

"They're amazed," she said after he was gone.

"About you?" Kyle spoke. "Well, that doesn't surprise me. I was amazed by you a long time ago."

She shook her head.

"Not just me," she said.

"What do you mean?" he asked.

"Both of us."

Kyle leaned forward a bit, and rested his hand on top of hers as he told her, "Look at what we've endured."

"We should be dead, Kyle."

"The Lord isn't ready to take either of us as yet."

"Maybe I would be better off dead."

Kyle snapped his hand away.

"How can you say that?" he asked angrily.

"I don't want to be a burden," she told him.

"To me? How could you be a burden? Was *I* a burden to you? Is that what you're trying to tell me?"

"*No!* Of course not, Kyle."

"Then I must know...what *are* you saying?"

"I'll never sing again."

"Why not?"

"Who would pay to see someone like me in a wheel-chair?"

"Anyone who has ever loved your music."

"I used to bounce around on stage, jumping up and down, and giving everyone a full performance."

"A performance may not be the real you."

"And what's the real me now, Kyle?"

"A remarkable human being who is going to keep her beautiful voice in shape and rethink her priorities so that she can go ahead and sit on stage in a wheelchair, showing all her fans that a singer's most important asset is her voice, not the athletic display she used to add in order to captivate everybody in the audience. The Lord will give a new power to your singing, Carla, and you'll reach many, many more people than ever before."

"If only I could believe that."

"Pray about it, my love. If it's of the Lord, it will happen. If not, it will be like a house built on sand, doomed as soon as the tide comes in."

"I love you, my dear, dear Kyle."

"God won't let us down," he added. "He has brought you and me too far for that. Lean on Him, and I'll do the same."

"You've always done that. It's more difficult for me."

"This time, we'll do it together."

He stood then, wobbly, yes, with more pain than he would ever admit to Carla but he was able to lean over the bed and kiss her lips with profound passion.

"Don't ever leave me," he said, sighing.

"Only God Himself can separate us!" she exclaimed.

Clapping...

Several interns, a nurse and some visitors were standing in the corridor, giving them a standing ovation.

Kyle blushed, then smiled appreciatively, and said, "Thank you for your encouragement."

And then he faced Carla again.
...we'll do it together.
There was no other way.

Epilogue

Nearly a year after Carla Gearhart Rivers was shot, the man whom police suspected of being her assailant was finally captured, and she was asked to identify him.

It had been an eleven and a half months that had changed her life and Kyle's. Their recuperation was never easy but nowhere near the futile ordeal that doctors had been predicting. In an ironic bit of timing, she would have to go from Nashville police headquarters to the opening of the largest entertainment arena in the city's history, apparently an architectural and acoustical state-of-the-art wonder.

"Can you do this?" Kyle asked as a new driver parked their new, specially constructed van in a designated spot near the back of the station house.

"I can, I want to and I will," she assured him.

Kyle no longer needed a wheelchair, and was able to walk with the use of canes. But Carla, while greatly improved, still needed an elaborate, motorized chair, which she had been sitting in rather than a regular seat during the trip from their home into the center of Nashville.

Kyle and the driver helped her out of the van.

Several members of the police department, including Chief Layton Forsythe, who was due to retire the following year, hurried out to greet them.

"It's a lineup situation, you know," Forsythe, white-haired, broad-shouldered, his face heavily wrinkled, told them. "He won't be able to see you at all."

Once inside, Carla and Kyle were taken to a small room with a large one-way window taking up two thirds of one wall. Walking into the adjacent room were six very rough-looking men.

Carla had no trouble making an immediate identification.

Chief Forsythe was pleased.

"I know you have an engagement at the new arena," he said sympathetically. "After you sign a couple of forms, I won't need to detain you both any longer."

"Chief Forsythe?" Carla asked.

"Yes, Mrs. Rivers?"

"Will you do me a favor?"

"Anything except hanging the guy from a gallows at noon tomorrow!"

"It's nothing like that."

"I was only kidding."

"I know."

"What is it that you want? If I can't do it, I'll make sure somebody else does."

"It's simple, really."

She glanced at Kyle. They had discussed her request, and knew that they were right in asking it.

"Tell that man something for me?" she said.

"Whatever you want," the chief promised, "word for word."

"Tell him," she said, smiling, "that Kyle and I forgive him."

"Forgive—" Forsythe said, stuttering. "You want to—"

"Yes," she said. "We both want him to know that he is forgiven by the two of us."

"But look what he put you through."

"Most people would spit at him, wouldn't they?"

"Or worse, Mrs. Rivers. Surely you'll think differently later."

"We won't," Kyle promised. "It's part of our faith. Without forgiveness, there would be nothing left."

The chief looked at them tolerantly but obviously annoyed.

"I'll see to it," he said.

"When?" Carla asked.

"Later, after you've left."

"Would you do it now, in that room, Chief?"

Forsythe nodded reluctantly.

After all the other men had left the room, and only Carla's assailant remained, Chief Layton Forsythe entered, and told the man what Carla had asked.

Then Forsythe returned to them.

"I gave it to him word for word," he said.

"What was his reaction?" Carla asked. "We couldn't hear anything. The speaker system must have been turned off."

The chief looked away for a moment.

"Was it so bad?" Kyle asked.

"No, it wasn't."

"Tell us then, please."

"He said that he would give up his life if that could have changed what he did. There were several times that he was close to suicide because of guilt. He deeply regrets everything and was going to ask us to tell you that he hoped you would come to forgive him in time."

"Do you think he meant it?" Carla probed.

"Yes, Mrs. Rivers, I do. He no longer seemed like a hardened criminal but a little boy somehow."

"I want to help him."

"That's going too far," Forsythe told her.

"There may be a chance to *reach* him, and I want to try. Our lawyer will be contacting you."

"But you already identified him. I hope you won't change your mind."

"I'm not going to. Is he wanted for other felonies?"

"A long list...robbery, rape, drugs, you name it."

"Then he needs a good lawyer."

"To get him off? That's generally what lawyers are supposed to do."

"To see that the system treats him fairly, and when he gets out of prison, to secure him a job and whatever else he needs."

"You really *have* forgiven this guy."

"Just as Jesus made sure my husband and I are being forgiven our sins daily."

Forsythe looked from Carla to Kyle.

"Remarkable," he said. "If only—"

Then he cut himself off before adding, his voice drained of emotion, "Let me accompany you outside."

After they were on the way to the arena, Kyle reached out and gently took hold of Carla's hand.

"I will love you for time and eternity," he said.

"Nor will I ever stop loving *you*," she replied. "I think I will walk again, yes, but if that is not what God has in store, I can face *anything* with you next to me. We may bark and yell and be angry or frustrated or whatever else. But that's to be expected. Nothing is going to hurt *us* from now on."

His lips touched her own, and they spoke nothing else until arriving at the arena, for what they felt, then, for one another, words would be useless, words could never express what their hearts were saying just then.

That evening, Kyle wheeled Carla out onstage before a

full house. She sang with such beauty and skill and power that, eventually, the band members had to stop playing and just listen to her while men and women in the auditorium wept row after row.

Then Carla and Kyle were rejoined and they sang a song that they had written together. It was called "Promises" and it told the story of how they were planning to live the rest of their lives.

This time the band played as never before.

* * * * *

Acknowledgments

First, I would like to thank Anne Canadeo for being a supportive and intuitive editor, one of the most astute I have worked with in more than thirty years as an author. She knows what she wants, and she is articulate, but she has the knack of not seeming arrogant. A writer is at ease with her.

Second, my appreciation goes to Randall Toye, an executive with a sensitive spirit and a friendly manner as well as a withering travel schedule that takes a special individual to endure and yet remain pleasant but, somehow, that is how he shoulders all his responsibilities, with good cheer and competence.

Third, I have no doubt that my wonderful new agent, Bruce R. Barbour, deserves some real applause. He is quite brilliant actually, a man with the keenest possible view of publishing and yet, despite all his knowledge and experience, he is very down-to-earth, a committed friend and business associate without whom my life would be poorer in all the ways that count. Getting the wrong agent can give you a hint of what hell is all about. Getting the right one gives you a glimpse of heaven. BRB is no ethereal angel of spirit only, but he may be God's messenger in purely flesh-and-blood form.

And, next, I want to thank my parents. None of the three of us is without imperfections but I am convinced that I have the lion's share of these. Knowing this makes me wonder how it is that they have ever put up with me over the years.

Finally, there are those hundreds of thousands of readers who have bought my *Angelwalk* series, as well as my other books. Without them, I would not be writing this latest novel.

Dear Reader,

I live on the outskirts of Hollywood and used to get into the various studios several days a week but even before living out here, I flew in frequently from New Jersey where I was born and raised. The projects were varied: a biography of Nancy Reagan; numerous celebrity interviews for a number of national magazines; pitching ideas for films to various studio executives; developing celebrity-based magazines with publishers in Connecticut and Virginia, and so on. I decided early on that I wanted to live in California instead of where I was, the grass-is-greener syndrome hitting me right between the eyes.

Twenty years ago, that was what I did, finally relocating myself from near-Atlantic City (a mere six months before gambling moved in and changed the city) to near-Hollywood.

I remember taking over silent screen star Valentino's former residence for an evening because one of my publishers wanted to throw a big Hollywood party. Well, he got his wish: we had more than eight hundred guests, fifteen security guards, twenty parking attendants; and some police officers outside to untangle the traffic mess on Benedict Canyon. In addition, there were numerous similar parties at my own home, attended by a list of major stars.

Heady days? You can be sure of that. And wonderful research for my latest book, *Promises*.

You will find a great deal of truth within the following pages, especially the impact that show business has on a large percentage of those who become involved. Not many are ennobled by it; but countless numbers are cheapened or destroyed. The long-range success stories are far outnumbered by the failures, in economic and/or moral terms. When preachers talk about "wickedness in high places", they usually mean Washington, D.C., as well as similar places of *government* power around the world. But that description is even more accurate when applied to the Hollywood centers of influence.

It has been this way since the days of the original movie moguls. And one could say, at some point, that the people making the films in this earlier era often led sinful lives but, at least, their product could be enjoyed, with some exceptions, of course. Today, though, a vulgar and unprincipled studio head greenlights a vulgar and unprincipled modern film, with its excesses of rotten language, nudity, grotesque violence and other questionable ingredients.

And now we come to Carla Gearhart, the protagonist in *Promises*. I have met countless numbers of people like her, fighting to stay on top, as the expression goes, and willing to do almost anything to achieve that goal.

But few of these stories end as Carla's does, nor is there the kind of joy along the way that she comes to know.

Roger Elwood

Available in December from

Love Inspired...

From the gifted pen of author

Lacey Springer

comes a heartwarming tale of
second chances and holiday joy.

CHRISTMAS ROSE

Abbey Wilson had fallen head over heels
for her boss. But Gabriel and Kendall had endured
more than his share of pain and simply couldn't bear
the thought of risking his heart again. Abbey knew it
would take the power of God's special love to
show Gabriel the joy his life was missing.

Could a miracle of love and renewed faith
be her very special Christmas gift?

Love Inspired

ICR1297

Follow the lives and loves of the residents of
Duncan, Oklahoma, in a heartwarming series from
Love Inspired...

by
Arlene
James

*Every day brings new challenges for young
Reverend Bolton Charles and his congregation.
But together they are sure to gain the strength to
overcome all obstacles—and find love along the way!*

**Watch for these titles in the
EVERYDAY MIRACLES series:**

THE PERFECT WEDDING
(September 1997)

AN OLD-FASHIONED LOVE
(November 1997)

A WIFE WORTH WAITING FOR
(January 1998)

WITH BABY IN MIND
(March 1998)

Don't miss any of these wonderful books,
available from

Love Inspired

Beginning in January from
Love Inspired...

FAITH, HOPE & CHARITY

a new series by

LOIS RICHER

Meet Faith, Hope and Charity—three close friends who find joy in doing the Lord's work...and playing matchmaker to members of their families.

Delight in the wonderful romances that befall the unsuspecting townsfolk of this small North Dakota town.

Enjoy the surprise as these matchmaking ladies find romance is in store for each of them as well!

Don't miss any of the heartwarming and emotional stories.

FAITHFULLY YOURS
January '98

A HOPEFUL HEART
April '98

SWEET CHARITY
July '98

Love Inspired

IFHC1

Dear Reader,

Thank you for reading this selection from the *Love Inspired* series. Please take a few moments to tell us your thoughts on this book. Your answers will help us in choosing future books for this series. When you have finished answering the survey, please mail it to the appropriate address listed below.

1. How would you rate this book?

1.1 ❏ Excellent   4 ❏ Fair
.2 ❏ Very good   5 ❏ Poor
.3 ❏ Satisfactory

2. What prompted you to buy this particular book?

_____

_____ 2,7

3. Will you purchase another book from the *Love Inspired* series in the future?

8.1 ❏ Yes—Why?_____

_____ 9,14

.2 ❏ No—Why not? _____

_____15,20

4. Did you find the spiritual/faith elements in this story to be:

21.1 ❏ Too strong?   .2 ❏ Too weak?   .3 ❏ Just right?

Comments _____

_____

_____22,27

5. Did you find the romance elements in this story to be:

28.1 ❏ Too strong?   .2 ❏ Too weak?   .3 ❏ Just right?

6. **What other types of inspirational stories would you like to read?**

   29 ❑ Mystery   30 ❑ Historical   31 ❑ Anthologies
   32 ❑ Humor   33 ❑ Nonfiction
   34 ❑ Other _____

7. **Where did you purchase this book? (choose one)**

   35.1 ❑ National chain bookstore (e.g. Waldenbooks)
   .2 ❑ Christian bookseller
   .3 ❑ Supermarket
   .4 ❑ General or discount merchandise store (e.g. K mart)
   .5 ❑ Secondhand bookstore
   .6 ❑ Other _____ 36,41

8. **Which of the following types of paperback books have you read in the past 12 months?**

   42 ❑ Contemporary popular women's fiction
       (e.g. Danielle Steel, Sandra Brown)
   43 ❑ Romance series books (e.g. Harlequin,
       Silhouette, Loveswept)
   44 ❑ Historical romance books
   45 ❑ Mystery
   46 ❑ Inspirational fiction
   47 ❑ Inspirational nonfiction
   48 ❑ Other _____ 52,57

   Inspirational Romance Fiction
   49 ❑ Heartsong   50 ❑ Palisades   51 ❑ Other _____ 58,63

9. **Please indicate your age range:**

   64.1 ❑ Under 18 years   .4 ❑ 35 to 49 years
   .2 ❑ 18 to 24 years   .5 ❑ 50 to 64 years
   .3 ❑ 25 to 34 years   .6 ❑ 65 years or older

Mail To:
In U.S.: "Love Inspired", P.O. Box 1387,
        Buffalo, NY 14240-1387
In Canada: "Love Inspired", P.O. Box 609,
        Fort Erie, Ontario, L2A 5X3   LINOV2B